Kye

Rise of the Pride (Book 6)
By
Theresa Hissong

All rights reserved. This book or parts thereof may not be reproduced in any form, stored in any retrieval system, or transmitted in any form by any means—electronic, mechanical, photocopy, recording, or otherwise—without prior written permission of the publisher, except as provided by United States of America copyright law.

Disclaimer:
This book is a work of fiction. Any resemblance to any person, living or dead is purely coincidental. The names of people, places, and/or things are all created from the author's mind and are only used for entertainment.

Due to the content, this book is recommended for adults 18 years and older.

©2018 Theresa Hissong
All Rights Reserved

Cover Design:
Custom eBook Covers

Editing by:
Heidi Ryan
Amour the Line Editing

Formatted by:
Wayne Hissong

Other Books by Theresa Hissong:
Fatal Cross Live!:

Fatal Desires
Fatal Temptations
Fatal Seduction

Rise of the Pride:

Talon
Winter
Savage
The Birth of an Alpha
Ranger

Book for Charity:
Fully Loaded

<u>Dedication:</u>
To the warrior inside every woman…

Contents:

Prologue
Chapter One
Chapter Two
Chapter Three
Chapter Four
Chapter Five
Chapter Six
Chapter Seven
Chapter Eight
Chapter Nine
Chapter Ten
Chapter Eleven
Chapter Twelve
Chapter Thirteen
Chapter Fourteen
Chapter Fifteen
Chapter Sixteen
Chapter Seventeen
Chapter Eighteen
Chapter Nineteen
Chapter Twenty
Chapter Twenty One
Chapter Twenty Two
Chapter Twenty Three
About the Author

Prologue

Nine months after the protests began

"How are you feeling, Evie?" Harold asked. The healer pulled the stethoscope from around his neck and placed it in his ears. He held the little disk out in front of Evie, but made no move to press it to her chest. Her anxiety over seeing him had eased over the past few years. Things had changed for Evie, but they weren't perfect.

"I'm fine," she sighed, nodding for him to go ahead and listen to her heart. "Are we going to check the damage again today?"

"Let me just give you a once-over, then we will talk," he replied, his voice soft.

It'd been almost three years since she had been abducted. Every few months, she'd come to see Harold, the pride's doctor, in secret. Besides her mother, he was the only one who knew everything about her time with the wolves. Thankfully, he upheld his strict policy about patient confidentiality.

"Take a deep breath," he ordered, pressing the disk to her back. She inhaled and exhaled as instructed, knowing he wouldn't find anything wrong with her.

She wasn't sick... No, what she had couldn't be

cured.

"Let's get you over to the ultrasound room," he said, smiling tenderly. "I'll take another look."

"Thank you," she replied, slipping off the exam table and following him into the other room. She knew this drill well and hopped up on the bed to begin rolling her shorts down so he could place the warm gel on her skin.

"Have you still been shifting several times a week?" he asked, clicking several buttons on the machine.

"Every chance I get," she confirmed.

"What about your back pain?" he continued as he finished preparing the machine.

"It doesn't bother me anymore since I started training."

"Have your cycles returned yet?" he asked, placing a hand on her wrist. When she looked up, she saw concern in the healer's eyes. He was an older male, his head and face clean shaven. His eyes were soft and caring, just as a healer's should be.

"No," she frowned. "Does this mean I won't be able to have cubs, doc?"

"Your body has been through a trauma, Evie. There was a lot of damage done."

"I appreciate your bedside manner, Harold," she began, pausing to take a deep breath, "but you are just placating me. I know that I'll more than likely be infertile for the rest of my days. Tell me the truth. I can handle it now."

"Evie," he sighed, pulling a rolling stool over toward the bed. He sat down and placed his elbows on his knees and steepled his fingers in front of his face. "As far as I can tell without opening you up for surgery, your reproductive system is intact, but the lack of your cycle concerns me."

"How?" she pressed.

"You have two months before you are matured," he replied, motioning for her to lay back so he could begin the exam. "When you finally become an adult female, I'm not entirely certain you will ever be fertile. Things could change for you and prove me wrong. We just have to wait and see. I want you to come for a check-up a few weeks after your birthday."

"I see," she said, looking up at the ceiling. A tear escaped and trickled down the side of her face. "Thank you."

"Would you like to stay and have a cup of coffee with me?" Harold asked, taking a moment to look over his shoulder at her as he worked on shutting down the machine.

"I need to get back to the house," she lied. "Mother is waiting on me."

"I'll walk with you," he offered, but Evie held up her hand.

"I have my gun," she informed him as she slipped on the special gloves Ranger had found for the women who were now trained to help protect the pride. Calla was still in training alongside her, but Talon had given permission for Hope and Evie to take care of security around his home when he or the Guardians were away.

"Be safe," he said, standing up from his chair. "I'll see you after your birthday."

"Thanks, doc," she replied, pulling the door open to leave the healer's office…knowing she had no reason to return.

Chapter One

Kye stood in the security room that housed all of the video monitors that recorded everything on their land and at the bar. Rain poured outside, the sound of thunder rumbling off in the distance, and he prayed it wasn't a sign of something ominous on his birthday.

The protestors that worked for the *Community* had mostly been rounded up by the law, and the government had stepped in to protect the paranormal community. That didn't mean the mercenaries associated with the *Community* had disappeared. No, quite the opposite. They'd become stealthier and more determined to take out shifters in any way possible.

The road in front of the pride's land had been cleared of humans six months ago. After the sheriff's department had placed deputies around their land, everything had gone quiet. That didn't mean the Shaw pride was safe. No, the deputies remained to that day, and all of the Guardians worked alongside them in protecting the pride. Officers patrolled The Deuce and one of the Guardians was posted inside whenever their doors were open.

Looking at the clock, Kye knew he needed to get to his brother's office. Today was going to be a long one, and even though he had been looking forward to this day for years, a little part of him wanted to just check on Evie instead. She'd been quiet over the past week, and he would readily admit he was worried about her.

"Happy birthday, brother," Talon announced as Kye entered the office. He'd wanted to avoid coming to see his brother this early in the morning, but he knew it was something he needed to do. He had turned twenty at the stroke of midnight, and it was time to take on new responsibilities.

"Thank you," Kye said with a grin.

"How are you feeling?" Talon inquired, raking his gaze over Kye. The assessment made him very uncomfortable. What was his brother wondering? It wasn't like he was going to automatically be more powerful than the alpha on the day he turned twenty.

"I'm feeling good," he smirked. "Why? Do you think I will become a raging asshole today?"

"You know that males who reach maturity tend to have some irritability." His brother was right, but the only thing Kye felt was stronger, bigger. The past few weeks, he'd been growing so much, he had to get all new clothes ordered when his thick arms no longer fit into his old cotton shirts.

"Yeah." Kye shrugged, standing up to stretch. "I just feel a little pumped up. I'm not sure what that means, but I sure don't have the desire to tear anyone's head off or anything."

"That's good," Talon chuckled, shaking his head. Kye saw his brother's shoulders relax as he rounded his desk.

"So, I guess we need to talk about my future."

"There will come a day when you will want to have your own pride," Talon said as he took a seat in the chair behind his desk. "You will need to learn everything you can before that time comes."

Kye watched his oldest brother and alpha of the pride thumb through a stack of papers on his desk. Each cub born to an alpha could carry the gene to become a leader. Between the three males born to their father, only Kye and Talon had grown to be rightful alphas. Their brother, Noah, had not, and from the sound of it, their middle brother was perfectly happy keeping his Guardian status forever.

"Where do we start?" Kye asked, sitting up straighter. "My maturity is here, but I don't feel the power yet." The power was magical in a sense. Talon could push his powers out to the pride and command them by combining that strength with his orders. Maybe he just wasn't feeling it because his mind was elsewhere…on Evie.

"You have powers, Kye," Talon pointed out. "I feel them when you are angry. I don't think you realize they are there."

"Really?" He smiled, feeling a little better at his brother's admission.

"Don't get cocky, brother." Talon rolled his eyes.

"It's a small push. Nothing like what I can do." To prove his point, Talon pushed out his powers. Kye whimpered when he felt his brother's magical strength.

"I see," he said, casting his eyes toward the ground, just as Talon's powers had demanded. Kye understood what his brother was saying. He obviously had a long way to go.

"I want to train with you for a few hours each day during the week," Talon stated. "I'd prefer we do this early in the morning."

"How early?" Kye frowned. He wasn't a morning person, but from the tic in his brother's jaw, he probably didn't have a say in it anyway.

"Six in the morning," Talon answered. "We can start tomorrow. Until then, go see your girl."

Kye used the dismissal to quickly leave his brother's office. He was expected to meet up with Evie in the training facility next to the Guardian dorm in an hour. He'd taken to training with her, but Ranger had expressed concern over his maturity.

Coming of age wasn't a simple birthday in their world. Being a shifter, the change usually caused the males to become somewhat wild. Kye had seen it with other males in the pride. Their tempers were short and they had a habit of scuffling with the other males at the drop of a hat. He didn't feel any different, but he wasn't going to take any chances with Evie. She'd been through enough in her life already.

"Happy Birthday," Evie purred as Kye nipped at her neck.

"My birthday doesn't count until you turn twenty," he mumbled, nuzzling the spot where he would mark her when they finally mated. The scent of his female was driving him insane. She was changing, maturing, regardless of the double braids she wore in her hair like she was still a young cub.

"We should celebrate tonight," she hummed, molding herself closer to his warmth when he wrapped one of the braids up in his hand, enjoying the feel of the silky strands.

"Not until we mate," he warned, wanting to kick himself for being so chivalrous. They'd waited this long to come together, they could wait two more months. *Right?* He wanted nothing more than to bury himself inside Evie's sweetness, but he wanted to do right by her because she'd been through so much in her life.

"You're killing me," she moaned.

"And you're not killing me?" he asked, following up his question with a thrust of his hips against her mound. His hardness was a blatant sign as to just how much she was wanted.

"Kye, please," she begged, pushing her breasts against his chest.

They were alone deep in the heart of the pride's land, choosing to get away from the pride when the weather had cleared. The bed of his truck was filled with blankets and pillows. The meadow was their go-to spot for when they wanted to be alone. How many years had they escaped to this place? Three? Four?

"You're making it hard to be a gentleman," he growled, nipping at her earlobe.

"I want to make love to you before we mate," she admitted, a soft blush painting the tops of her cheeks. "I'm afraid of it hurting when our beasts take over."

"I'd never hurt you," he frowned, cupping her face. "I'll be gentle, promise."

"The other mated females talk about their first mating and said that their mates are…demanding." She sighed. "I want to be prepared for that time, Kye."

"We will take it slow," he vowed, taking her lips with his.

His female. She was strong and patient, willing to learn how to overcome the things she'd experienced at such a young age. Kye was proud of the woman she was becoming.

"What if we're not mates, Kye?" she asked, biting her bottom lip.

"We've talked about this," he reminded her.

"Are you sure?" she pushed, reaching for his

hand. "What if we are not mates, and someday, you find the one who was meant for you?"

"I will never want anyone else," he swore, leaning over to take her lips. "You are mine forever, Evie." She nodded but didn't say anything else for the longest time. He wrapped his arms around her and just held on tight.

There was always a possibility that they were not fated to be together, and he was being honest when he said he wouldn't want anyone else. Evie was his end game. She was it for him, and the thought of another woman in his arms made him feel a sense of disgust. No one would ever hold his heart as much as Evie did. There was no question about that.

"Want to run with me?" he whispered against her lips. He needed to change the subject.

"Of course," she sighed.

"Not much longer," he promised, pulling his shirt over his head.

Nudity was never an issue within the pride, and Kye had seen his mate's beautiful body many times before, but as she undressed, his heart thundered in his chest. His panther snarled in his mind to give her what she'd been asking for…right now. He pushed his beast back, ordering it to calm the fuck down. There was plenty of time to show her all the ways he wanted to worship her on their mating night.

The panther bucked, but submitted as Kye let the cat free. Evie's beast appeared and sat on her haunches. She was so much smaller than him, and his protective side wanted nothing more than to keep her by his side, but that wasn't Evie. No, she huffed and looked toward the woods, digging her nails into the dirt and racing for the cover of the trees.

Kye's panther chuffed, sounding almost like a laugh as he followed her scent. His keen eyesight scanned the area as they ran, watching for any signs of enemies. He wanted her safe, no matter what.

They ran for a while, finally passing over the old fence-line and into the new land his brother had purchased months ago. This new area was secured, and some of the Guardians had already made trails through the woods for the pride to run and play. The one place that they'd all fallen in love with was a huge pond right in the middle of the new property.

Most days, there would be several of the pride gathered at this place, shifted and playing in the water. Thankfully, today, the place was deserted. Kye's panther stopped at the edge of the water and shook his head when Evie's made a running leap onto a tree that hung over the water's edge. Her panther looked over its shoulder at him, then jumped in, making a huge splash. Her head came up above the water and she floated there for a moment before slowly making her way out to the center of the pond.

He dropped down on his belly, stretching his paws out in front, but kept his hind legs tucked under him in case he needed to jump into the water for any reason. His panther didn't move from his spot as he watched his potential mate swim casually in the center. The sun was out and Evie's animal relished in it by closing her eyes and just floating.

Kye continued to scan the area, his nose twitching with each new scent. He knew there were a few rabbits on the other side of the pond, because their smell drifted on the soft breeze. A hawk sat high up in a pine tree to his left.

For the next hour, Evie played by herself in the water, not once making a move to get out or to ask him to join her. It didn't matter to Kye, because he was relaxed and enjoyed watching her not being on edge for once.

Three years ago, she wouldn't have left the house unless it was necessary. The training she'd been doing with Ranger and himself was strengthening not only her body, but her mind as well. It was one of the hardest things for Kye to accept, but he had.

His panther growled low in its throat as the scent of males approaching crossed his nose. Their heavy footsteps registered shortly after. His beast snarled when he saw some of the younger males enter the clearing. They all froze as they caught sight of him, taking a moment to set their fishing poles on the ground.

"Hey, Kye," one of the boys called out. "Mind if we…oh, sorry." Ellis, one of the young boys, blushed as he picked up his pole. He started to back away, but stopped at Evie's human voice.

"It's okay, Ellis!" she hollered from the pond. His mate had shifted and was swimming in her human form. "I'm done here anyway."

Kye's upper lip raised as he stood from his perch. The beast inside him wanted the boys away from his female, even knowing her nudity wasn't going to bother anyone. But on the other hand, Ellis was sixteen and just starting his hormonal flux as his body gained weight to become a fully-matured male over the next four years. It was their world's answer for puberty. So, Kye was sure this kid was knocking one off left and right as he watched porn late at night in his bedroom down the hall from his parents.

"It's fine, Evie," Ellis stammered, looking nervously at Kye. "We can come back later."

Before Evie could say anything else, the boy grabbed his things and left them alone, his friends following quickly after him. Kye's panther relaxed after the younger males had gone. He raised his nose to sniff the air just to make sure. When he swung his head around, Evie was starting to come out of the water, her body bare as a human.

Kye wanted nothing more than to shift and pull her into his arms, taking the time to show her how much he truly loved her, but he wanted to do right by Evie in all ways. Sadly, it would have to wait for a little while longer.

"I'm going to shift and head home," she said.

"Run with me?"

Kye's beast climbed to his feet and let out a soft cackle, letting Evie know that he would go wherever she asked. His girl smiled warmly and began to shift. At the same time, a flash of light caught his eye off in the distance. Kye moved quickly to place his body in front of Evie's, only relaxing slightly when he caught the sheriff's scent. When the male came into view, Kye's heart stopped in his chest. Sheriff Lynch's eyes were wide with fright.

"Get the hell out of here now! Humans are on your land," he warned. "Run!"

Chapter Two

Ember stood tall, holding her hands up toward Talon. He immediately picked her up as she babbled her baby nonsense. The alpha knew his daughter wanted his attention. It was something that he'd never tire of when it came to his family.

Looking over at his mate, Talon wondered when they'd have another child, but with the way of their current world, he wasn't sure he wanted to bring another life into the dangers they were facing. The *Community* was still at large, gathering up shifters of all species, locking them away in cages and experimenting on them like lab rats. The government was raiding these facilities as fast as they could find them, but it was hard.

Only a few of them were able to call out to their alphas for help, giving locations in their hysteria while being held as prisoners. Others weren't so lucky. Word had come that the ones being found couldn't call out to their leaders because the *Community* had learned about the alpha's ability to speak mentally with their people, and they'd killed the alphas before taking the prisoners for study.

The Guardians of the Shaw Pride were even more protective of Talon than ever. He was a ball of anger with them staying so close, but he understood their worry. He was worried, too.

"She needs a nap," Liberty yawned. "In fact, so does her mother."

"Go rest, my love." Talon smiled, but it didn't reach his eyes. He knew his mate felt his unease by the way she softly closed her eyes and released a quiet breath. She looked over her shoulder at Booth, Storm, and Dane, who were posted at the entrances to the room, standing at attention. Dane and Booth were at the one closest to the foyer, while Storm leaned against the frame leading into the kitchen. All three males watched the windows and doors that led outside.

Talon waited until his mate was out of the room before taking a seat in the high-back chair by the fireplace. He was safe from any windows at his back, and he used that time to place his head into his hands. There was a sense of unease in his body, almost like a small vibration.

Talon!

His brother's call jerked his body upright. The Guardians were immediately at his side. He didn't have a chance to answer his brother before the message came through.

Sheriff just appeared by the pond to warn us that humans are on our land. Evie and I are coming to the house.

"Humans are on our land," Talon snarled. "Kye and Evie are on their way here from the pond."

"Talon, we need you in the security room," Booth urged as Talon stood from his seat.

"I'm going after my mate and my daughter," he growled, feeling his beast push at his human skin. The three guards made a triangle of protection around him as he moved toward the stairs. They quickly reached the alpha's bedroom and Liberty gasped when Talon rushed into the room. "Safe room, now!"

Liberty didn't question him. She just scooped up Ember and found her place at his back. The Guardians made their protective triangle around him once again and they were on the move. Each step was coordinated. It'd been planned and practiced months before when the threats had originally come for the shifters.

"Shhh, little one," Liberty cooed to their daughter who was crying from being woken up suddenly.

"Inside," Booth barked, pushing into the control room. The room was as secure as a bank vault and it was the new safe haven for the pride in the event of an attack.

Noah jumped to his feet as soon as they entered, immediately pointing at one of the cameras. "Someone get the back door. Evie and Kye are almost here."

Talon saw his brother and the young female racing up the road that led to the mated cabins, turning for the backyard of his home. Dane hurried out the door. His image was picked up on the interior cameras as he reached the back door. He held it open for the two cats to enter.

Talon sent out a message to his pride, warning them of the breach. His command for them to hide was sent back with fear from the pride. He sent out his calming touch through their connections, but it didn't help. Feeling his pride on edge sent anger surging through his veins.

"Find out who is on my land!" Talon roared as he felt a ripple of fear come directly from Savage, who was out on patrol. Everyone froze when gunshots rang out.

"Talon?" Liberty cried, reaching for him when his eyes flashed amber and his canines appeared in his mouth. "Talon!"

"I want Guardians in the woods, now!" he barked as he closed his eyes tight. "Someone find Savage. He…he's been shot."

Evie laid on her side as she panted heavily. Kye had already shifted and left to find clothes. She had no desire to move until he returned. Her panther was exhausted from the run they'd just completed. The Watcher had appeared and yelled at them to run because there were humans on their land, and that had sent fear down her spine. When would they ever feel safe again?

Dane was standing guard at the back door, a gun strapped to his hip. Kye rushed back down the stairs with a pair of sweats and one of his cotton shirts in his hand. Evie shifted and climbed to her feet slowly, accepting the clothes.

"You two should go into the safe room with the alpha's mate," he said, not taking his eyes off the backyard. Kye grabbed her hand and started to turn, but froze when gunshots rang out in the air.

Everyone in the house gasped as their enhanced hearing picked it up. Feet pounded from the security room. Some Guardians shifted while some stayed human. Talon growled at Kye as he looked at Evie, "Get my mate into the safe room!"

Both of them ran down the hallway, meeting Talon at the door to the room. Evie pushed past her alpha and went straight for the weapons closet, stopping to scoop up the keys to the lock from the desk. No one questioned her when she reached inside and found a pair of gloves and a handgun she was comfortable handling.

"What are you doing?" Kye growled, his eyes flashing between his human and animal form.

"I'm protecting my alpha's mate and the next alpha to our pride," she replied, keeping her heart rate calm, just as she'd been taught in all of those hours of training. Evie donned a shoulder holster and secured one gun, reaching in for another one. She tossed it to the alpha's mate. "Come on, Liberty."

Evie closed and locked the door to the weapons and reached up above the frame. A soft click sounded and the door opened again to reveal a room behind the closet. It was a fairly large space and held several cots and blankets. A refrigerator sat in the corner that held enough water for a damn army.

Liberty scooped up her daughter and rushed into the room, a look of determination on her face. "Lock me in."

"You know the drill." Evie breathed deep and nodded toward Liberty, closing the door as soon as possible. She quickly wrapped her braided hair into a bun and secured it with a few hairpins she kept hidden in her hair. She double-checked the door and gave it one solid knock to let Liberty know she was secure.

The room had been added on months ago, giving the pride a place to hide in the case of a breach on their lands. Talon had hoped it wouldn't be needed, but they all knew at some point they would.

"I'm shifting and you stay with me," Kye ordered, lifting the shirt over his head. "I mean it, Evie. Don't leave my side."

"I won't," she growled, feeling her own beast prowl in her head. "I know what I'm doing."

"Evie," he began, but a hard glare from her shut him up. He quickly dropped his pants and shifted, coming up to nudge her side and nip at her wrist. Evie knew he was going to protect her. It was in their nature, but she was ready to fight alongside her pride to keep everyone safe.

"Let's go."

Noah nodded at them and reached up to kill the lights in the room. Kye and Evie stepped out the door and waited for it to close. The sound of the bolt sliding into place signaled that Noah was now protected with Liberty and Ember. He would be the first line of communication with Talon and the other Guardians.

Evie removed her gun from the holster and held it at her side as she walked silently down the hallway, past the alpha's office. Kye's panther huffed softly when they came to the opening of the living room. She felt his warmth as his body touched her right leg.

The house was silent, but that didn't mean it was empty. When she looked to her left, Axel, the new Guardian, was poised at the door, his eyes flashing between amber and icy blue. The Guardian nodded toward the back door where she saw Lucky Cooper in place. She held up one finger and pressed it to her lips. With a deep breath, she pointed upstairs, letting them know she was going up to clear all of the rooms.

Kye stayed beside her as she moved to the bottom of the stairway. Axel covered the front door and Evie caught herself praying no one decided to shoot through it as she passed. Thank god, because she really didn't want to know what getting shot felt like anytime soon.

She took the stairs one at a time. Kye's beast crouched low to the ground as if he were stalking prey. His huge body made no sounds as it moved over the hardwood flooring on the upstairs landing. He was a predator…they didn't make sounds when on the hunt.

Slowly, they cleared all of the rooms and returned to the foyer where the young Guardian was waiting. No words were spoken, only a short nod of her head to let him know the alpha's home was secure. It was time to wait out the threat and pray that the ones who got onto their land were caught.

Chapter Three

Savage cursed as he was struck in the shoulder by a bullet. His panther snarled deep inside his mind, demanding release, but that wasn't going to happen anytime soon. The wound would heal, so he didn't need to shift right away. No, he wanted to take out the human who'd shot him on an even ground. He wanted the male's blood his own way.

"Show yourself, you fucking coward," Savage called out, allowing his panther eyes to scan the area. There was nothing. No scent, no sounds.

The scent of his own blood tickled his nose, but he pushed back the burning pain. His feet made a rhythmic sound on the forest floor as he ran in the direction he thought the shooter had been. He shifted his eyes and ears just enough to use his beast's heightened senses.

Bang!

"Motherfucker!" Savage dropped to his right knee when he felt a bullet rip through his thigh. Looking down, the blood was oozing out of a spot about halfway between his hip and knee. Thankfully, the dumbass shooter missed his bone.

"Stop fucking shooting me!"

A movement straight ahead caught his eye, and

the scent of a human male reached his nose at almost the same time. With a snarl, Savage pushed himself to move, but the pain in his leg was too much. Damn, he wasn't going to go out like this. No, he had to keep his pride safe from this asshole.

His panther ripped from his skin, shaking off the change. In his shifted form, the wound began to heal, but not quickly enough for him to run at full strength. Only the thought of this male getting to his mate and babe pushed him forward.

Savage rounded a tall shrub and saw him. The male was tall, muscular. He wore all black clothing and a ski mask. In his hand, he held a pistol as he ran quickly toward the back of the property.

Where are you?

His alpha's voice pushed into his mind. Savage replied, telling him he was not far from the old fence line. A few seconds later, the sounds of his leader and brothers arriving caused a cat-like smirk to pull at the corner of the panther's mouth. This human was as good as dead.

Bang!

Everyone scattered as the male turned and fired off a shot that went wild, hitting the trunk of a tree. Savage's beast wanted this ended... and now. With a push of his hind legs, he climbed a tree and used the large branches to get himself up higher.

Herd him back toward me.

Talon must've conveyed the message to the other

Guardians because they all split up and made a wide berth, circling the male. When he realized he wasn't going to make it to the fence, the shooter doubled back the way he had come.

Savage's beast calculated the perfect time to pounce, taking the human down as soon as he was near, but the human rolled out of his grasp. The male screamed out when Savage's claws dug into his thigh, taking flesh away from the bone. Talon was calling to him, telling him to leave the human alive so they could question him. He'd obey, but that didn't mean he wanted to. Savage regained his footing and started to leap for the male, but the human put the gun to his temple and pulled the trigger.

The back door flew open and Talon stepped through with anger on his face. Evie gasped quietly at the distress coming from her alpha. Behind him, Storm, Ranger, and Taze looked equally pissed off.

"Is my mate and daughter safe?"

"Yes, sir," Evie answered, looking toward the hallway where the safe room was hidden. "We've had no problems here at the house."

"The land is clear and the male who shot Savage killed himself before we could get answers," Talon snarled, his eyes completely amber.

"How's Savage?" she asked.

"He's with the healer now," Talon replied as he marched past her, but stopped and turned around on his heel. "Thank you."

"You're welcome," she replied, watching her leader walk away.

Kye's body shimmered as the shift from his beast made him human again. He stood and pulled her into his arms. "You did well, Evie."

"Thank you."

Kye kissed her forehead and followed his brother. She was sure he was going to find his clothes. Within minutes, a sense of calm filtered through her, and she saw the Guardians visibly relax. Talon's mate must've calmed him, and thankfully, was okay.

The house began to fill up with pride members. Her mother entered holding Landon, Savage and Mary Grace's little boy. She immediately came to Evie's side.

"Any word?"

"No, mama," Evie answered, but she didn't look at her mother. Her eyes scanned the pride, wishing they weren't so afraid.

"Can you take Landon for me? The females are going to start making food for everyone. I'm sure the alpha will want everyone at the house tonight."

"Let me return my gun to the security room."

"Take your time," Marie replied, reaching out to

squeeze her hand. When Evie looked at her mother, she saw pride and relief in her eyes.

She left the front room, stopping at the door to the security room. She knocked twice and looked up at the camera above the door. A click sounded when someone inside released the lock, allowing her entry.

She slipped into the room, noticing how Talon was holding Liberty and Ember close while he scanned the monitors next to Noah and Kye. Evie didn't say a word while she returned the weapon and holster to the hidden room. She didn't need that one, because she usually kept one in her bag or on her person, but since her and Kye had shifted to run in the woods, she had been without her protection.

"Evie?" Liberty called out as she turned to leave.

"Ma'am?"

"You did a great job." Liberty smiled, hiking her daughter higher up on her hip. "Thank you."

"No problem," she said as she smiled warmly. "I'm going to watch over Landon until we hear something. My mother and some of the other females are going to make a meal."

"I'll be out shortly," Talon vowed. Kye looked up from the monitors and winked at her as she headed out the door.

Evie returned to the kitchen and took the baby from her mother. Little Landon was only nine months old, having been born on Thanksgiving night the year before. He was such a stout baby too, already strong like his father. Savage had been such a proud papa when Landon came into the world.

It took about an hour before the females of the pride had food on the tables. The males stood back and waited for everyone to make their plates before getting their own. Evie watched as her pride gathered together, talking quietly while they waited on word about Savage.

"We are going to increase patrols on the land for the next few days," Kye announced as he approached. "Liberty isn't allowed to be at the bar, so Dane is going to be there full time from now until this is over."

"We all need to be careful," she said, transferring the baby to her other hip.

"You're a natural with him." Kye smiled at the little boy.

"Ah, thanks," she stammered. Turning her head, she didn't want Kye to see the sadness on her face. She still hadn't told him about what the healer had said, and she didn't think she could. It wasn't the time or the place, anyway. For now, she'd push that information to the back of her mind.

The back door opened and Savage entered with his mate, Mary Grace. She looked exhausted and worried. The male came straight for his son, taking him from Evie. "Thank you for watching over him."

"He's a great baby." Evie tried to smile, but it didn't reach her eyes.

"You okay?" Savage asked.

"Yeah, just a little uneasy." She shrugged, hoping the half-lie wasn't detected by the Guardian. "How are you?"

"Perfect," he winked. "We're going to be okay. This will pass."

"I hope you're right," Kye said, wrapping his arm around her waist. The connection was welcomed as the sun was setting on a disastrous day.

The rest of the Guardians arrived not long after, their expressions masked for the sake of the pride. It was no secret that they'd disposed of the body in the woods. She was sure the sheriff had a hand in making the man disappear.

"Where's the sheriff?" Evie asked. She'd expected him to be around since he was the one who had warned them of the human on their land, but he'd been scarce since it all began.

"He's coming," Talon answered as he entered the kitchen. "We *will* get to the bottom of this, and I want everyone on rotation until this is over. It may take some time, but I refuse to let this cult, or whatever the fuck it is, destroy us."

Sheriff Lynch's heart beat at a gallop as he drove through the gate at the entrance to the pride. Two of his deputies were on duty and nodded as he passed. The entire situation with the male entering the pride's land was as messed up as could be. The human male was sent by the *Community*, but Garrett had no damn clue that the fucker was going to kill himself when he was caught.

The Guardian Booth was at the door when he knocked. He had his hand on a gun at his waist, but didn't have it drawn. Booth nodded and stepped aside, his face somber as he spoke. "Talon's in his office waiting for you."

"Thank you," he replied and turned down the hallway. It was hard to not look at the members of the pride as they watched him with all of their icy blue eyes. It didn't matter that he didn't know all of them very well. It was his task to keep them safe, and he'd become very drawn to them all over the past few years. The thought of something happening to the pride honestly scared him. Not because if they were gone, he would be too, but because he really cared.

"Give me an update," Talon ordered as Garrett entered the office.

Storm and Kye were at their leader's side, both with their arms folded over their massive chests. The alpha's baby brother had filled out over the past few months. Nearing his twentieth birthday had been a time of growth for him and, from what he'd been told, Kye was to be an alpha one day.

"The *Community* had made a last second decision

to send in that human male to try and kill as many as he could before he was caught. My vision happened within minutes of warning your brother and Evie."

"So, what? They waited to tell the male what to do until after he was at our fence?" Talon frowned. "That makes no sense."

"Does anyone else know about you?" Storm asked, his eyes flashing amber.

"No." Sheriff Lynch shook his head. "You are the only ones. Why do you ask?"

"Could they've known you have visions and are working with us?" Storm ran a hand through his short-cropped blond hair, cursing when Garrett shook his head again.

"I'm unknown to everyone except the pride," he promised.

"Then how?" Kye asked, his brow pushed forward.

"I do not know, but I will find out," he stated.

"What about the male killing himself when he was caught?" Kye continued, dropping his arms and placing them on the desk next to where Talon was sitting. "They had to have known something for this male to off himself."

"My only guess right now is that they don't want to be caught for some reason," the sheriff answered. "In wartime, an enemy is trained to kill himself to keep from being tortured for information. This is the only reason I can come up with for now."

"Has the *Community* made a statement?" Talon asked.

"No, they've been too busy scrambling for cover since a new lab was raided just a few hours ago."

"Where?" Kye asked.

"About a hundred miles outside of Phoenix, Arizona."

"Shit," Talon cursed. "How many facilities do they have? And how long have they been setting this up?"

"That's what I want to know, along with the fact that I only started seeing visions of them coming for you now that the threat in North Carolina has been eliminated."

"Are you sure they are not working with other paranormal entities?" Kye asked, his panther growling behind his words. "Is this why you didn't know anything until the human crossed over our land?"

"I really don't know, but I'm going to find out," Sheriff Lynch promised.

Chapter Four

Evie punched the heavy bag in the Guardians' training room. She was solely focused on making every hit count. It was just after sunrise, one month to the day after Savage had been shot, and she knew she'd have a few hours to train before Kye was out of a meeting with the alpha. He'd taken on more roles within the pride since the breach, and had been learning everything he could in the event that he'd have to take over the pride in the future.

The door to the facility opened and Evie glanced out of the corner of her eye to see Hope enter with a bag slung over her shoulder. Ranger followed a few seconds behind, dropping his own bag on the bench.

"Good morning," Hope greeted, kicking off her shoes. "Where's Calla?"

"I'm here!" Calla called out as she rushed through the door, out of breath and already sweating. The young female had her short, blonde hair tied back with a black bandana to keep it out of her face. "I decided to take a long run through the woods."

"By yourself?" Ranger frowned. Evie cringed when Calla looked at him with narrowed eyes. The *Community* was still on the hunt for their kind, and even with the heightened security, the alpha wanted everyone to be in pairs when out of their homes.

"I was fine," she bristled. "I have my gun." The young female turned around, lifting her tank top to reveal a holster sewn into the workout pants she was wearing. A pistol was secured in place at the middle of her back.

"The *Community* is still out there," Ranger warned, looking at all three women. "I know you're training, but these guards they've trained are showing no mercy when it comes to rounding up shifters. Have you not been watching the news? Do you not remember what happened last month?"

"I have, and I do remember," Calla replied, dropping her eyes to the mat. "I'm sorry."

"Come on," Ranger said, backing down just a little. "We need to do some training before I have to go into work."

News reports were full of the *Community* rounding up shifters and the government raiding their churches where the shifters were being held. From the looks of it, some of the buildings had been turned into prisons, and the conditions were terrifying.

Just two nights ago, a breaking news story had come out, saying that they'd found another lab where some of the shifters were being held and studied in California. The pride had gathered around the television in the alpha's home to watch them pulling out several body bags of the deceased.

Evie tried not to let all of the news reports get to her, knowing that what the *Community* was doing was just as terrifying as what the wolves had done to her. It tested her strength more so than anything since she'd been kidnapped and tortured.

A wolf with a collar in his hands.

"Bitch!"

His boot as he kicked her in the belly.

The needles that gave her sedatives.

Evie squinted her eyes and shook her head, trying to clear the memories. Her PTSD was still present, and it was something she was probably going to have to deal with for the rest of her life, but that didn't mean she wasn't going to survive. She'd come this far in her healing process, and there was no way she'd go back to those dark days.

"Evie?" Ranger called out, pausing as he approached. The large Guardian stepped up to her side and lowered his voice. "What's going on?"

"Nothing," she answered, shaking the thoughts from her mind. "Nothing at all."

"Do you want to sit out today?"

"No," she scoffed. "I'm not leaving."

"Fine," he replied, handing over a set of gloves. "You can spar with my mate today."

Hope approached and waited for Evie to prepare for their training session. She took a swing and missed Hope. Cursing, she held her ground as the female struck out against her. Bouncing on the balls of her feet, Evie tried to concentrate, but it wasn't working.

Evie tried not to let the worry seep into her mind while she trained, and for the most part, she succeeded. Until a memory flashed through her mind and she lost focus for a split second.

"She's bleeding."

"Good! That'll keep 'em from making more."

"Oh, poor kitty, don't cry. We're doing you a favor."

"Evie!" Hope hollered, rushing to her side. Evie didn't even realize she was flat of her back until she opened her eyes and saw Hope, Ranger, and Calla standing over her.

"Sorry, sorry," she said, trying to sit up. Her jaw ached a little from the blow Hope had delivered.

"You lost focus," Ranger growled.

"I know!" she snapped, tearing at the Velcro straps on her gloves. She tossed them to the side and looked up at Ranger. "We done?"

"Yeah, but you better be here in the morning," he warned as she grabbed her bag and made a move for the door. "I'll walk you home."

"Don't bother," she bit out through her clenched teeth. "I'm fine."

The hot September breeze coiled around her body as she stopped at the edge of the building, taking a few deep breaths to calm her beast. The memories would always be there. It was just when they struck out of the blue, Evie couldn't stop the flashes that ran across her mind's eye… and that was when she would be set back. That was when she would regress back to that scared and defenseless girl from so long ago.

Fabric tore as her panther took control, shifting in a blink of an eye. Claws dug into the dirt at her feet as she fled for the forest behind the alpha's home, knowing she shouldn't be alone, but at that moment, she just needed to run.

Dane stood with his back against the end of the bar closest to the door, his foot crossed over his ankle. He appeared relaxed and with no cares in the world, but what others didn't know, he was on guard. His eyes scanned the crowd and his nose was alert to every scent that drifted through the bar. He was in charge of security at the door of The Deuce, acting as the first line of defense against any enemies who might try to cause trouble.

Human deputies, wearing plain clothes, ate lunch and played pool as if they were any other average Joe in town. Cole Bryant was behind the bar, a pistol strapped to his hip and a shotgun secured under the bar. Noah was at the pride house, monitoring the cameras with a keen eye. The security and fire-power in the bar was as good as any military installation, and everyone who worked there had been trained in the event of any trouble from the *Community*. Even Moe, the cook, was armed in the kitchen.

Winter was sitting at the bar with Ranger at his side. Luke, the other bartender, was washing glasses at the sink. Both Guardians were watching their mates as they worked at The Deuce. Liberty had put her foot down about the bar, refusing to close its doors during the protests with the *Community*. Talon had fought her decision and put up quite the fuss of his own, but in the end, his mate's wishes were granted.

"Want a beer?" Cole offered as he leaned against the inside of the bar.

"Sure," Dane nodded, watching Cole when he reached into the cooler to grab a beer. The bartender was a little older than him. For a human, he was almost as large as Dane. He'd served in the human's military and got out after a few tours overseas. He had a small scar on his upper lip that made him desirable to the women who came to the bar. Yeah, Dane had noticed them flirting with him, but the man kept to himself and did his job, rarely giving the women his time. Unlike Dane with his longer hair to cover his mangled ear, Cole kept his deep brown hair cut high and tight.

"Liberty is conducting interviews today for another waitress." Cole rolled his eyes, setting the beer in front of Dane. "I'm sure this is going to be fun."

Dane lazily reached for the beer, accidentally

touching the tips of Cole's fingers. A shiver of awareness rolled through his body, and he frowned. That was very strange. The feeling wasn't magical enough to call to his beast, but it was definitely something. Maybe he was just on edge? Whatever it was, Cole hadn't felt it, because the male moved over to take an empty beer bottle off the bar top to toss in the trash can like nothing had happened.

"Yeah," Dane said, clearing his throat. "Winter is going to sit in with Liberty for her protection. We don't trust anyone these days."

"Agreed, my friend," Cole said with a nod. Dane tipped the bottle toward Cole as sort of a thank you before taking a drink. When the bottle leveled out, the door to The Deuce opened and in walked the most beautiful blonde female Dane thought he'd ever seen.

"Damn," Cole whispered under his breath. Dane had to agree. Since he was closest to her, and in charge of security, it was his job to check this woman out. *It'd be my pleasure.*

"I'm here for an interview with Mrs. Shaw," the woman said, her emerald green eyes assessing him in that way that males loved. "My name is Olivia Stone."

"I believe she's expecting you," Dane replied, his eyes scanning her face and trying his best not to stare at her breasts or thick hips. He failed, and miserably, at that.

Fuck! She was stunning. Long blonde hair, big

green eyes, and breasts that would fit his palm perfectly. She smelled of sunshine... and she was human.

"I'm a little early," Olivia stammered.

"No, I think you're right on time," he flirted, holding his hand out toward the bar. "Why don't you have a seat and let Cole make you a drink while I have someone get Mrs. Shaw for you."

"Thank you," she said with a smile, a light blush dusting her cheeks when her eyes traced his outstretched arms and the mass of muscles there. Yeah, that right there was what men loved; to have women look at them with lust in their eyes. Even his panther sat up in his mind, purring softly at her.

Cole leaned against the bar with a naughty smirk on his face, asking her if she'd like something to drink. It wasn't like the bartender to show much interest in the ladies. *Interesting.* So, this change was enough to make Dane raise a curious brow at the male who was putting the charm on the same woman he had only seconds before. Dane waited for his panther to snarl at the other male flirting with the female, but the beast didn't. He still panted with interest at the two of them flirting. In fact, he liked watching them. Dane was known to have a certain taste in his pleasures. Seeing those two together was one of them.

Cole told Luke to cover the bar, and then he escorted the female toward the back office by placing his hand on her lower back. Dane's upper lip lifted, wishing he could touch a female as easily as the human males did. Being a shifter, you touched women, but only to fuck or to see if they were your mate. Either way, most of them at least wanted to get to know the females first.

Dane had touched plenty of women, but mostly for a hot night in the sack. He didn't care much for finding a mate. Now wasn't the time to be bringing a female into their world. It was best that he stay single and stop looking at sexy, blonde females.

Yeah, right.

Chapter Five

"Explain to me why you ran off from training alone," Kye bellowed as he came upon Evie lying in a thicket right at the edge of the meadow they went to often. She was in her panther form, her eyes closed as she growled low in her throat. The beast's tail swished back and forth, letting Kye know she was agitated.

When Ranger had called him, Kye immediately knew where she'd run, and he didn't use his panther to go after her. He knew that she'd probably need to see him... just him. It was obvious that she'd had some type of bad flashback from what Ranger had told him.

"Evie!" His panther was growling in his mind, but he wouldn't let the beast free to show comfort toward hers.

"You used to talk to me about what was going on," he reminded her. "Now, all you do is train."

Nothing. She wouldn't shift. At that moment, he wished he had his brother's ability to force her to change. He needed Evie in his arms.

"Please, Evie... let me take some of this pain from you," he whispered, knowing she heard him. He sat on the ground and opened his arms, praying she'd accept him.

Her panther looked over at him, closed its eyes, and stood. Kye waited patiently for what felt like hours before the beast climbed into his lap. A shimmer signaled her change, and within seconds, Evie was curled up on his lap, tears pouring down her face.

"I need to tell you what happened with the wolves," she cried, "and when I do, you are going to have to make the decision if you're still going to want me."

Kye's heart shuddered at her words. How in the hell would anything she had to tell him change his feelings for her?

"Evie," he began, using his forefinger to tug at her chin. "Look at me. What's going on?"

"I don't even know where to start," she sniffled, wiping her eyes. Kye's heart broke into a million pieces at seeing her tears, and he wanted nothing more than to just hold her so no one else could ever hurt her again.

"Start at the beginning," he urged, keeping a tight hold on her.

"I was coming from the alpha's home and heard a strange sound by the side of my mother's house," she began. "I don't remember all that happened other than a man grabbing me. He smelled so bad…"

Evie paused and shivered. Kye kissed the top of her head, hoping to give her strength. He didn't know how he was going to sit there and listen to her recollection of what had happened without losing his mind, but he had to be strong for her.

"I screamed, and that's when he put a cloth over my mouth," she sighed. "I woke up to a boot in my ribs and a busted lip."

"Fuck," Kye whispered, holding her tighter.

"I tried to shift, but the pain in my neck stopped me," she said, touching the spot where they'd collared her with a leather strap imbedded with spikes. "They laughed at me and said that if I completed the shift, my panther and I would die."

"My brother showed me the collar," Kye admitted, remembering how viciously angry he was the night she was found. "It was designed to kill a shifter."

"The wolves make them," she added, looking up at him with big, icy blue eyes. She wasn't crying, but there were unshed tears building. It was only a matter of minutes before they escaped.

"I'm so sorry, baby," he cooed.

"Every time I would wake, they'd have fun kicking me," she admitted. "The two wolves that were there to watch over me liked to taunt me to call out for Talon. If my panther would push forward, they'd attack me. She wanted their blood."

"She was trying to protect you," he said softly.

"After the second day…"

"Evie?" Kye called her name. She'd recessed into herself like she was ready to shut down. "What happened?"

"After the second day," she repeated, looking up into his eyes. "I won't hate you if you decide not to touch me when I turn twenty."

"Why are you saying that?" he growled, his mating scent thick in the air. She was scaring him. What could've happened that was so bad she was willing to let him go?

"Kye," she whimpered, wrapping her arms around herself protectively.

"Tell me," he begged. "Evie, you're scaring me."

"They… they kicked me and punched me in my stomach so hard, I started bleeding like I was having my cycle," she hiccupped. "They saw the blood and they both laughed, saying they'd done me a favor so I couldn't bring anymore cats into the world."

"Those motherfuckers!" Kye exploded, jumping to his feet to pace as she scrambled away from him. Evie covered her face and began to cry harder as she rolled to her knees.

"I'll more than likely never be able to give you cubs, Kye… I'm so sorry."

It was still dark outside when Kye's eyes fluttered open. Evie was snuggled against his side, and thankfully, she was still asleep. Her pain had filtered into his dreams and turned them into nightmares.

Those wolves had hurt her more than he had imagined. He really couldn't fault her for not telling him. Was he mad? Yes, but as his brother had ordered, Kye wasn't going to lash out at her. The news hurt, knowing he would probably never be able to breed an heir to his own pride someday. No children to carry on the alpha gene could be disastrous. Their species could die out without a leader.

Evie shifted in her sleep, and he rubbed her hair to soothe her enough that she eventually relaxed and fell back into a deep sleep. Kye watched her through the soft moonlight that peeked through his curtains. He didn't need the light, but he appreciated his panther resting for the first time since he'd been told what had happened. Kye needed his human side right now.

He had to assure her for an hour that he would love her regardless of her ability, or inability, to have cubs. In the end, it didn't matter. Kye only wanted Evie.

She'd brought up the elephant in the room, as well.

What if they were not fated to be mates? How would they be able to continue to love each other ten years down the road? Was he being an asshole when he thought about how he didn't care for another female? That the woman of his dreams was already here?

The kidnapping, the protests, and the *Community* were driving a wedge in what was once their secret world. Kye remembered growing up with no fences... no borders to their freedom. Now, everyone in the pride was told to stay in groups and to listen to the Guardians when they spoke of anything dealing with their safety.

Hope, Calla, and Evie were trained in firearms so they could help protect the pride. The alpha's mate and her sister, Nova, were experts and had no worries when it came to training the female pride members. If their ancestors could see them now, Kye wondered what they'd say.

Traditions and rituals were still enforced, but were they truly needed?

With the change of their existence being known to humans, even having something as simple as a Fall Equinox shift could be dangerous for all of them.

Kye pulled Evie toward his chest and closed his eyes tightly, praying to the gods that she would be safe. She just *had* to be. No one should have to go through what his girl had gone through at such a young age.

Chapter Six

Liberty handed Ember off to June, promising to be back as soon as possible after her training session with the other females was done. Evie, Calla, and Hope had found their calling in life by pushing themselves to learn how to protect themselves.

Liberty snickered to herself when she thought of the discussions she'd had with the alpha late at night and after the baby was asleep. Thankfully, Talon had kept an open mind when it came to her stance on letting the females at least try. He'd growled all alpha-like when she told him she could protect herself.

Having been human once, she had relied on her knowledge of self-defense to keep her and Nova safe when they'd left the bar in the wee hours of the morning. She thought of her dad and how he had religiously trained both of them on handling firearms.

Nova had been training with them on occasion, and had even helped Liberty with teaching the females how to use guns. Liberty and Nova were splitting their time working at the bar, and it didn't leave much time for anything else since their cubs were born.

She opened the back door and stepped out, a

warm breeze washing over her. It was early September and you'd think it was still July by how hot it was outside. Fall couldn't come fast enough.

"You ready?" Hope asked as she stepped up on the back porch to the alpha's home.

"Let's go," Liberty replied, closing the door behind her.

When Liberty and Hope entered the training room, Evie was sitting on the bench with her elbows on her knees. She was staring off at a spot on the wall and didn't look up to acknowledge Liberty at all. The young female was lost in her thoughts, and it broke Liberty's heart to see her still dealing with what had happened to her.

"I need to talk to you," Evie whispered so low that even Liberty's enhanced hearing almost missed it. Hope froze as if she wasn't sure she was supposed to be included. "It's okay, Hope. I'd like to talk to you, too."

"Okay," Liberty said softly. She set her bag by the end of the bench and took a seat next to Evie. She reached up and ran her hand over the young female's blonde hair. It'd grown so much over the years. She wasn't the cute little girl she used to be. No, Evie had grown into a beautiful young woman who was on the cusp of her prime and possible mating with her brother-in-law. They'd be sisters soon, and that thought made Liberty smile. "Whenever you are ready."

"We are here for you," Hope said, kneeling down in front of Evie.

"I told Kye exactly what happened to me," she began, pausing to take a deep breath. "I haven't told anyone but my mother and the healer. They'd kept it a secret because I asked them to, but I couldn't lie to him anymore."

"Oh, honey," Liberty sighed, pulling Evie to her chest when the female began to cry. Liberty held her for the longest time, just letting her get out her emotions. Hope placed a comforting hand on Evie's knee, and they just waited for her to stop crying long enough to tell them what was on her mind.

It was a private moment, and one that she was sure Evie didn't want anyone else to witness. Ensuring that they were not bothered, Liberty allowed herself to partially shift so she could send a silent message to the alpha, begging him to keep the pride out of the training room. He didn't ask her for details and she felt his strength bleed into her. He was worried, but knew Liberty would come to him if she needed him.

"I want you to know," Evie sniffled, lifting her head from Liberty's chest. Liberty folded her hands and placed them in her lap, showing the female that she would be patient with her.

"We are here for you," Hope repeated as she sat cross-legged on the floor at Evie's feet.

Liberty didn't have to wait long before Evie went

into detail about how the wolves would kick her in her stomach and back whenever she was awake. They knew she'd call out for Talon and they *enjoyed* torturing her until they got tired of it, knowing their blows were so painful she wouldn't be able to concentrate long enough to call for her alpha. They'd finally sedate her when they were done. She bled for days as if she were having her cycle. The males found it funny and would joke about how she'd never give birth to cubs. She was humiliated.

"What has the healer told you?" Liberty asked.

"I may never have cubs," Evie cried. "I told Kye I wouldn't fault him for not mating me."

"I am so sorry," Liberty cooed, pulling Evie back to her chest. She wiped her own eyes, feeling this female's pain as if it were her own. That was what Talon had told her about being the alpha's mate. She'd have to be there for the pride in their times of sorrow and happiness.

It amazed Liberty how Evie had kept herself together all this time and Talon not knowing anything through the bond he shared with the pride. Or did he? Did he feel her pain and sadness? Did he know through his connection to them that this female was suffering?

"Oh, Evie," Hope cried, wrapping her arms around both the females.

"Why haven't you and Ranger started a family?" Evie mumbled against Liberty's chest. Liberty had wondered the same thing. Usually, mates had their first cub within the first year, but so far, Hope and Ranger had remained childless.

"Well," Hope sighed, reaching up to tuck Evie's hair behind her ear. "Ranger and I have decided that we don't want to have any cubs right now."

"Really?" Evie gasped, pulling away from Liberty. They were shocked at Hope's confession, but Liberty kept her expression neutral.

"There's no written rule that says we have to have cubs, Evie." Hope shrugged. "It's not that I can't have them. We just use protection when I'm fertile."

"Oh!" Evie blushed. "I really didn't want to hear that about Ranger. He's like my brother."

"Sorry," Hope apologized, shrugging when Evie's shock subsided and she giggled. "Really, Evie. You have all the time in the world to work on a family with Kye. There are other alternatives that the humans use. I'm sure our kind can do the same. Harold is smart. He'll help you."

"I don't know what to do," Evie whispered.

"We are going to get you through this," Liberty promised, nodding to Hope over Evie's head as sort of a thank you. "The pride will hold you up when you can't do it yourself. We are a family, Evie. This is what we do."

Talon rubbed at the center of his chest. He felt his mate's pain, but he already knew why. Evie must've finally confessed why she'd been hurting since she had been kidnapped. Talon had known. Hell, he'd felt her pain from the moment she'd been found and those damn sedatives had worn off.

For three years now, Talon had been softly sending the young female his strength through the magic that connected them. He had no idea that she'd take up learning to fight with Ranger to help her heal, but she had, and he was so proud of her for it. There was no way to tell if she had made that decision on her own, or if his slight push of power had something to do with it.

He'd never known exactly what had happened, and he was sure that he never would. The healer hadn't spoken a word of it to him, and he wouldn't ask. He knew Evie would come to him in time, but what he didn't expect was his brother sitting in the chair across from him raging mad once he found out.

"I want to kill them all over again!" Kye exploded out of his chair, standing up to pace. His eyes were completely amber and his canines were thick in his mouth. The skin on the backs of his arms was rippling with the need to shift.

"It is over, Kye," Talon reminded him, sending out a calming presence, but his brother surprised him by pushing back with power of his own.

"Stop trying to calm me!"

"You're losing it, Kye," Talon calmly stated.

"Do you blame me?" he snarled.

A knock at the office door caused Kye to sit heavily in the chair when Talon moved to answer it. He only unlocked and pulled the door open a few inches before walking back over to his desk and leaning against the edge. Kye looked over his shoulder and groaned, "Is this really necessary?"

"You need us, baby brother," Noah said as he took a seat next to him.

"What I need is for my girl to be free of her demons," Kye whispered, shaking his head. Talon knew he was trying to push away his panther, and from the amber glow to his eyes, he was struggling.

"She's strong," Talon answered. "What you need to do is be supportive. Don't go off the rails in front of her. She doesn't need to see this." Talon made a motion to indicate Kye's current state.

"I would *never* hurt her," Kye growled, raising his head.

"We know this, but you are maturing," Noah said. "I'm worried your temper will get the better of you."

"I swear to you both. I will be okay." Kye paused, raising his hand to stop Talon from cutting in. "I mean it, Talon."

"What I was going to say," Talon gritted his teeth and leaned forward, "is you can come in this office to yell, scream, and do whatever it is that you need to do to get your frustrations out, but as your alpha, I'm ordering you to not lose your temper in front of that female. Evie needs you to be there for her when she falls."

"Okay," Kye sighed, not pushing back against Talon when the order was given. "Okay."

Talon gave the order and Kye would have to obey. The magic he had over his pride was so strong, his words were law. He could drive them to destruction or calm them to the state of near-death, but he wouldn't. Talon considered himself a compassionate man, and the idea of making his family into killing machines sent fear through his heart.

"May I go now?" Kye asked, pulling the alpha back from his thoughts.

"Yes." Talon nodded, but held up his hand to stop his baby brother. "I'm here if you need me."

Kye nodded and left without a word to Noah, pulling the door closed as he left. Talon took a seat and rested his face in the palms of his hands. Noah moved silently and took the seat Kye had vacated. When Talon looked up, his middle brother had the same look of worry on his face.

"That girl will be okay," Talon said aloud. "I won't let her fail."

"She's an asset to this pride," Noah agreed. "Evie may be more powerful than we think."

"Her skills are as good as the Guardians." Talon scowled. "What the hell am I going to do if one of these females want to fight in the summer for Guardianship?"

"You let them," Noah shrugged.

"Against a male?" Talon asked. "What if Evie wants to become a Guardian at the Solstice next year? Kye will be fighting for his spot then. Am I going to put them against each other?"

"Damn." Noah shook his head. "We would have to find another female to join for the fights to be fair."

"Right now, Hope is the only other female," Talon chuckled. "I know our females are strong and our males are mostly accepting of their training, but could you imagine the discord in our pride if two females step into the circle?"

"I'm sure Ranger and Kye will be in distress," Noah replied, running a hand through his dark hair. "Good thing you have nine months until then."

"Which reminds me," Talon said as he looked toward the window. "The Fall Equinox is next week. We need to start making security plans for the pride during the ceremony."

"I can work on that for you," Noah offered.

"Please," Talon said, his mind drifting to his mate. "I'd like to have the night off to spend with my mate and daughter."

"I'll call a meeting with Winter and Savage for later tonight." Noah stood and extended his hand to

Talon. "We will come to you in the morning with a plan."

"Thank you," the alpha sighed. "I appreciate it."

Chapter Seven

It felt good to tell them.

Evie held out her hands while Hope wrapped them so she could take out some frustrations on the heavy bag. Liberty had left not long after she'd had her breakdown and talk with the alpha's mate. Having Liberty know was freeing. Hope was as close as a sister to her, too.

"Where's everyone?" Hope asked as she secured the end of the tape.

"Calla and Taze will be here soon," Evie answered. Calla had been hanging around that male a lot lately. It was odd, because Taze had given all of the females so much trouble in the beginning, but now, he was one of their biggest supporters. He'd taken to Calla after the final straw had broken and Taze was almost stripped of his Guardianship by the alpha.

"That's a weird pairing," Hope chuckled, then stood from where she had been sitting on the ground in front of Evie.

"Tell me about it," Evie said, rolling her eyes. "Calla swears there's nothing going on."

"I think Malaki had something to say about that." Hope frowned.

"He will come around," Evie hoped. "He's very protective of his sister."

The door opened, quieting their conversation. Calla and Taze entered, both of them smiling. Just like all of the males, Taze was so much larger than Calla. His body could shield her if the need ever arose. He'd let his hair grow out on top, but he had kept the back undercut and shaved tight to his scalp. His icy blue eyes glowed from the contrast. Calla kept her blonde hair up in a bandana most days, preferring not to have it in her face. Evie understood the need. The wolves liked to use that to drag them around when they were held hostage.

"Evie?" Calla whispered as she approached.

"I'm fine," she promised, shaking her head slightly. "My mind wandered for a second."

"I know the feeling," Calla sighed, reaching out to take Evie's wrapped hands. "We are going to beat this."

"Yeah, we are," she agreed, looking at the door when it opened.

"Hey," Kye said as he walked in. His eyes immediately fell on her, and she felt his love from across the room. "Are we ready to train?"

A collective agreement sounded and they got down to work. Calla and Hope paired up as Kye approached her. He didn't say anything as he stopped a few inches away. He tucked a finger under her chin and gave it a little nudge. When she looked up, he pecked her lightly on the lips and gave a wink. "Let's see what you can do."

Kye donned the focus mitts and turned toward her. She held her fists up in front of her face and waited for him to nod, giving her the okay to begin. She jabbed with her right hand, making the perfect connection. Their eyes were locked on each other and she felt an overpowering connection to him. Each time she hit, he would nod and softly say, "Good."

The sound of her knuckles meeting the mitts was one of the most comforting sounds she'd ever heard. Each and every time, it told Evie that she was winning the fight against her demons. She'd done this on her own. No one had forced her to learn to fight, and it'd been the one thing that was solid in her life since that night.

"Focus," Kye barked, bringing her thoughts back to the present. He didn't stop her. He didn't ask her what was wrong. All he did was hold those mitts up to remind her where to send all of her energy.

She punched with her right hand, feeling a small thrill as Kye was pushed back a few inches from the strength of her blow. The next one, he held his ground. The third, fourth, and fifth time, the force sent him back a step. Before she knew what had happened, Evie relaxed and leaned back, signaling she needed a break. When she finally broke eye contact with Kye and looked around the room, she noticed they'd worked their way to the other side of the mat. Her strength had done that, and everyone in the room had stopped what they were doing to watch.

"You did well, baby," Kye beamed.

Everyone parted and started cooling down after their training. The door opened and Dane walked in, searching the room. Evie felt his worry when his eyes fell on Calla. "Your brother is looking for you, and he's not happy."

"What the hell is his problem?" Taze barked, taking a protective stand next to Calla.

"His sister," Dane answered as he rolled his eyes. "I'm here so he doesn't cause any trouble. The little punk has been quite irritating, and I figure if he starts something in here, I can tell the alpha that we were training."

"Please don't," Calla gasped, stepping around Taze. "He's going through a lot right now."

"Like?" Evie pushed, moving to her friend's side.

"Well, he just turned twenty three months ago, and I've been fighting." Calla shrugged and bit her lip. "I think he wants to try to fight for Guardian status next summer."

"Unless we have new members come into the pride, he will have to fight me," Kye stated. "He needs to be training."

"He's running on anger and hatred," Calla explained. "I've moved out of the alpha's home."

Everyone gasped at her confession. Hope came over to take Calla's hand. "She's staying with Ranger and me for a little while."

"Is it that bad?" Taze asked, his eyes flashing amber. "Why didn't you tell me?"

"I didn't want anyone to make a big deal about it," she frowned, the blush of embarrassment reddening her cheeks. "He's going through his maturity. I'm sure he'll settle down in the next few months."

Dane tsked, looking out the back door. "Well, you can either stay or head out the other side of the building, because he's coming."

"I'd rather go," Calla said, looking up at Taze. "Will you walk me back to Hope and Ranger's place?"

"Get your things," Taze ordered, but Evie could tell he wanted to stay. The young Guardian seemed very protective of Calla, and she was sure that Taze would give Malaki a beat down if he disrespected his sister.

"You two need to go," Dane urged, pointing to the back door of the building.

Both of them left only seconds before the door flew open and one pissed off male entered the room. "Where's my sister?"

"She's not here," Dane said, leaning against the wall as if he were bored. "Might want to tone it down a bit. The attitude is causing problems around here."

"Man, fuck you," he snarled.

"No, fuck you," Dane growled, pushing away

from the wall. "Little boy, you don't want none of this."

Malaki launched himself at Dane, but was quickly brought to heel when the Guardian used his strength and training to subdue the maturing male. "Let me go!"

"Wrong move, asshole," Dane laughed. Evie cringed when his fist connected with Malaki's face.

Harold tied off the last stitch to Malaki's eyebrow. Sometimes, the damage would require a stitch or two for a day, and from the beat down Dane had delivered, this male needed it. Patching up Guardians was his specialty, but these young ones were getting more and more heated as they matured. The one in front of him was already on his last nerve.

"Boy, don't you know not to cross a Guardian?" the healer scolded, turning to drop the bloody gauze in the trash can behind him. He grabbed a stool and pulled it away from the wall to sit down and maybe talk some sense into the kid. When he turned around, he saw the young male's eyes had turned amber, his jaw set.

"They've turned my sister against me," he stated.

"No, they didn't." Harold sighed, shaking his head. "Boy, your sister is learning to fight alongside the other females for a reason."

"There's no reason why she needs to learn how to fight," he scoffed. "It's my job to protect her until she mates. After that, her male will keep her safe."

"You have a lot to learn about females," Harold laughed sarcastically.

"What do you know?" Malaki asked, a smirk turning up the corner of his mouth. "You've never been mated."

One minute, the healer was sitting in his chair. The next, he'd moved with super speed to take the young male's throat into his hands. His claws extended and nicked Malaki's flesh.

"I may not have a mate, but I have had a mother and three sisters," he snarled. "They're dead because they didn't know how to protect themselves, and the Guardians weren't there in time to save them. I'd have given anything to go back and teach them how to fight, but I can't because it's too late. Do you want that to happen to Calla? Huh, boy?"

"I'll be with her," he choked out when Harold squeezed tighter.

"You cannot be with her all the time," he barked. "She is strong, and you're putting her at risk by causing problems. That young female cannot concentrate on getting stronger when all you do is treat her like she's a fragile doll. Have you seen her fight?"

"N…no," Malaki stuttered when Harold's

canines thickened in his mouth. This little punk ass kid was going to make him break his rule of not doing damage to a pride member that he'd have to later put back together.

"She can take down a Guardian," Harold informed him, putting his nose against the male's. "God, you make me sick. Be respectful toward your sister, and if you come back into my office with injuries from getting your ass kicked again for being a jackass, I swear to the gods, I will let your little punk ass bleed out on my doorstep."

Chapter Eight

The following week, Evie sat at the desk in her room, holding a calendar. Her birthday was in two weeks. She'd finally be twenty, and the first thing she wanted to do was run directly to Kye when she opened her eyes that day, but he had other plans.

A note was on the doorstep of her parents' cabin that morning. The paper was made of thick, beige parchment, and there was a red string wrapped around it. Her mother excitedly pushed Evie to the door so she would be the one to pick it up.

"Go in your room and open it!" Maria, her mother, giggled.

"I'm going!" Evie smiled as her mother gave her a little push.

She'd climbed on her bed and pulled at the end of the string, loosening the bow. Carefully, she removed the letter inside, opening it to reveal a handwritten letter from the love of her life.

Evie,

Please do me the honor of meeting me in the meadow tomorrow for lunch. My brother Noah will escort you at exactly noon.

Until then,

Kye

Evie folded the letter and held it to her chest. What was he up to?

She blushed hard, wondering if he was finally going to give in and make love to her before they mated. Did it really matter this close to her birthday? The more she thought about having sex with him, the more nervous she became.

"What is wrong with you?" she mumbled to herself.

She was a strong woman, and had been learning to fight for herself. Why did the idea of being intimate with the love of her life send her into a giggling fit of a teenager? How hard could she roll her eyes before they got stuck that way?

"Well?" her mother asked from the doorway.

Evie looked up and smiled warmly. A tear welled up in her eye and, before she knew it, she was sobbing like a damn baby.

"Oh my, Evie," her mother gasped, rushing to her side. "What happened?"

"He…he is so sweet," she laughed, holding up the letter for her mother to see.

"Oh, daughter," Marie said, pressing a hand to her chest. "You scared me."

Her mother read the letter and smiled, setting the paper aside to pull Evie into an embrace that was one she'd come to find more comfort from recently than she ever did as a child.

Marie was in her late fifties, her hair was kept long and the blonde from her youth had turned into a beautiful white color. Her father still told her how beautiful she was... just like the day they'd mated.

She wanted that with Kye, regardless of what fate had planned for them.

"What if we are not mates?" she asked after several minutes.

"There's no rule that says you have to wait for your destined mate," Marie said. "I've known several couples who never had the spark and still lived their lives as if they'd been chosen for each other by the gods."

"I don't want another male, mama," Evie said, wiping her face. "God, I hate crying."

"It's normal," Marie chuckled, wiping a motherly hand down Evie's hair and tucking the locks behind her ear. "You are about to go through a change of your own."

"I hope it's for the better," Evie grumbled. "Things are still... bad with the healer."

"Give your body time, sweet girl," Marie replied, touching Evie's flat stomach. "Everything happens for a reason. Mother Earth knows what is best for us. Trust her to guide you. Whatever her will is, accept that, my child. You have years left to think about children. Mate that man and love him before anything else."

"Have you talked to Jon?" Evie asked, changing the subject. Her brother had moved to a different pride when he'd taken a job with them in Nebraska.

"Yes," her mother nodded. "He said he loved his new job, and he would have time to come home during the holidays."

"I kind of miss him," Evie admitted. Her brother had always been a loner, but he was sincere. She wished that he'd stayed, but the offer was too awesome for him to pass up. He wasn't wanting Guardianship within the Shaw pride, and moving was something he yearned to do.

"We do too," Marie smiled, "but he's happy, and that's all I want for my children."

Kye was nervous as hell, waiting for his female to arrive at their meadow. Noah promised he'd escort her there so she'd be safe making her way through the woods. It didn't matter that she could protect herself. The fact that a human had gotten onto their land and was able to get close to her set him on edge.

Kye wasted time looking over the items he had placed on the blanket. He'd made a lunch fit for a queen... his queen. The selections were her favorites; fried chicken, potato salad, rolls, and enough chocolate chip cookies to feed an army. Okay, most of those were for him, but she loved them almost as much.

The wind blew softly through the tops of the trees. Summer was coming to an end, and a few leaves had already fallen from the trees despite the warm temperatures. It didn't take much longer for Evie's scent and the sound of her soft footfalls to reach him. When he turned around, Noah was standing next to his girl at the opening to the meadow. He whispered something to Evie and nodded before leaving without saying another word.

"Hey," she blushed. "You did all of this for me?"

"Of course," he replied, taking her hand and leading her to the blanket. "Hungry?"

"Starving," she said, a smile lighting up her face.

Evie took a seat next to him and kicked her legs out so she could rest on her elbows. Kye watched her as she tilted her head back to soak in the sun that was shining down on her beautiful face. His heart swelled to the brink as he waited for her to come back to him.

"Sorry," she apologized. "The sun feels good on my skin. Colder weather is coming, and I don't like it much unless I've shifted."

"I know," he said, remembering the first winter when they'd started a relationship. She'd been cold as they took a walk through the woods, and he had given her his coat. She still had it to that day and Kye would never ask for its return.

"Can we eat?" she asked, eyeing the spread of

food. "You brought cookies?"

Kye nodded and handed her the food, waiting until she started eating before making his own plate. They spent the next hour snuggling on the blanket, petting each other. He could kiss her every moment of every day for the rest of his life and die a happy male.

"I need to work off some of this energy," she stated, helping him pack everything away.

"Do you want to run or head back to the dorms and spar?"

"Spar," she said, standing up. Kye caught sight of her ass in the tight jeans she wore, and tamped down his need for her. They'd have time to explore each other in just a couple of weeks.

As they stuck to the trails leading back toward the alpha's home and the Guardians' dorm, Kye passed his mother's home, stopping at the short driveway that led to the garage. "You know this will be ours, right?"

"Is that what you want?" she asked, looking up at him. Concern flashed across her features, but only for a split second.

"I'd love to have you live there with me," he said truthfully.

"I'd be honored to call it ours." Evie leaned up and kissed his lips, taking a moment to cup his face as she stood on the tips of her toes to reach him.

"Come on," he said, taking her hand away from his face reluctantly. He didn't release her as he started walking, moving aside as a few cubs ran past them on the road.

Evie stopped at her family home to grab her bag and change clothes. Kye waited patiently on her porch and then they headed to Talon's place when she was done. After leaving the leftovers in the fridge, they headed over to the gym in the dorms, finding Storm, Dane, Ranger, and Hope inside.

"Let's spar," Kye suggested, watching the others do the same. Storm and Dane were on the ground, fighting for dominance, and he knew that Evie was starting the same training with Hope a few days a week. He wasn't ready to do any floor work with her until she was stronger. The thought of her getting hurt by him because he was easily more than two times her size left a bad taste in his mouth. He could accidentally hurt her, and he'd never forgive himself if he ever left a mark on her skin.

Chapter Nine

Soldiers stood with weapons strapped across their chests at the entrance to the underground facility. The island off the coast of Maine was considered private property, and the *Community* was banking on that to keep them off the radar. With over two hundred acres of wooded area, the scientists would be able to study the shifters in the wild. An underground bunker was used to house them when it was time for the experiments. The home was a disguise for them, and the strict security protocol ensured that no authorities would be sticking their noses into the research they were doing to prove the shifters needed to be eradicated.

So far, they'd captured several black panthers, a few black bears, two wolves, and one small female coyote. Their research began to take a turn when they realized that the ones they had captured were dying after several weeks in captivity. After some harsh interrogation, they found out that the species only lived with the blood of a leader, an alpha. The most exciting, and puzzling, information they'd discovered was that these creatures could live with the blood of *any* shifter leader.

The young female bear shifter they'd captured finally confessed right before she died that they had to drink the blood of an alpha to stay alive. It didn't take long before the scientists found a leader and brought him to the island, forcing the others to take his blood. The others had been alive for four months so far with no signs of sickness. This gave further proof to their theory that any of the species could possibly breed outside of their own kind.

Now, the breeding program would begin... as soon as they found more of the creatures to study.

***

"An entire pride has been found deceased in upstate New York," Sheriff Lynch barked into the phone as soon as Talon answered.

"What?" Talon gasped, feeling his panther whine inside his mind. "How? What happened?"

His ass hit the chair as Garrett went into detail about how a delivery driver reported finding bodies all over a property he'd delivered packages to two days earlier. Upon further investigation, it was found out that it was a pride of werepanthers, very similar to the Shaw pride.

"What was their name?" Talon choked out, worried the pride was one that his father had dealt with in the past.

"Theo McCormick owned the land and home, but he has yet to be found," the sheriff said. Talon could hear him shuffling papers around on his desk. "Did you know them?"

"Yes," he growled. "Theo was an old friend of my father's before he died. So, there's been no sighting?"

"None."

"Someone has taken him," Talon offered. "Where was his son? Eros?"

"He's deceased," Garrett reported. "He was the only one that was murdered. The others died of natural causes."

"Then Theo has been taken," Talon snarled, slamming his hand down on his desk.

"How do you know this?" Garrett pushed.

"Because if the alpha is taken, and the rightful heir is not there, the entire pride will die."

"We believe the *Community* has him," Garrett said, then lowered his voice, "but no one has found him yet. Their compounds are drying up with each raid. The government is looking, Talon, but I don't know what's going to happen. I need you to keep your people accounted for until we get more information."

"We have our security plan in place," Talon grunted. "Why haven't you seen any visions regarding these shifters being taken by the *Community*?"

"Because," Sheriff Lynch paused to take a deep breath, "I'm here to protect the Shaw pride and no one else."

Talon cursed and closed his fist, trying his best not to punch the desk that sat in front of him. It was his father's, and one that Talon had remembered playing under while his father conducted pride business when he was just a small cub. It would be passed down to his daughter someday. He didn't want her to have to deal with the hatred and horrors of the current state of affairs.

"You call me if you have any other information," Talon ordered, hanging up on the lawman.

Talon sat in silence for several minutes, trying to calm his worry, knowing the pride would feel it if he showed any distress. Sometimes, it sucked being an alpha and having the magic inside of you, but he wouldn't ever give it up. He needed his pride as much as they needed him.

Instead of sending out a call to his Guardians through their link, Talon sent a text message off, requesting a meeting in his office in an hour. He had a few minutes to go check on his mate and cub before they arrived.

"Hey," Liberty whispered as he met her in the hallway. She'd just left their daughter's room, closing the door silently. "She's finally taking a nap."

"Does this mean I get my mate for some uninterrupted time?" he teased, pulling her small body flush against his. She hummed low in her throat when his erection pressed against her stomach.

"I do believe we have some time," she flirted, giggling softly when he picked her up and tossed her over his shoulder, caveman style.

He'd get lost in his mate until it was time to inform his Guardians about the new information provided by the sheriff. He just prayed the *Community* didn't come for them, and he was relying on that Watcher to do his damn job and keep his family safe.

The pride began gathering at nightfall. The Fall Equinox was upon them, and Evie was nervous with all of the problems with the humans. The Guardians were posted all over the land, and Noah was in the security room with Dane at his side. They were monitoring the cameras with keen eyes, but that still didn't make them feel at ease.

Talon was inside his home with Liberty and his cub, Ember. Food had been made for the pride, but not much of it had been touched. Evie had forced herself to eat, knowing she would need the energy to shift at midnight.

Thankfully, this ceremony would be short. No new cubs or matings had happened since the summer, and that meant Talon would only give a speech before commanding everyone to shift. They'd run and return to their homes before sunrise.

"Tonight is going to go smoothly," a voice said from behind her.

Evie gasped and turned on her heel, placing a hand on her gun, only to relax when she saw it was the sheriff. He was in plain clothes, not his angel wings. He just looked like a normal human, but he didn't smell like one. No, he had a sweet scent to him that was more than comforting.

"You promise?" Evie asked, hoping he was right. The sheriff was something unlike her and her family. He was a Watcher, an angel of sorts, and he'd been tasked by the gods themselves to keep the Shaw pride safe from humans. Just like when he'd showed up in the woods to send her and Kye running back to the alpha's home.

"I promise," he smiled warmly.

"Can I ask you something?" Evie blushed, biting her lip. Maybe, just maybe, he could tell her that she and Kye were, in fact, mates. Maybe he'd know if she'd ever have cubs in the future.

"I cannot tell your future, Evie," he guessed, or had read her mind. She really didn't know how he knew, but she wished he could tell her something.

"I was hoping that maybe…" she paused.

"I wish I could tell you everything you are mulling over in your head is for naught, but I am not at liberty to say what will happen. My job here is to keep you all safe. Just know that you will be okay.

That, I can promise you."

"Even with the *Community*?" she asked.

"There will be a time when you need me," he said, then winked. "Just remember… you can always call for me." The sheriff nodded and disappeared with a soft flash of light.

As much as she wanted the answers immediately, she knew the Watcher was right. She should wait and see what fate holds for them. By the gods, she didn't want to wait. Evie wanted to know now.

Kye had been more loving toward her since she told him the news. The picnic in the meadow was the sweetest thing he'd ever done for her. The fact that they went straight to the training room to spar sent a thrill through her that she knew was her arousal at his attention.

There were times when they'd be working on jabs and upper cuts, but all she wanted to do was drop her gloves and beg him to mount her. The thought of that made her blush. Why did fighting with him make her as hot as the soft kisses and touches in the meadow?

"Hey," Kye announced as he came up behind her, wrapping his arms around her waist. He kissed the spot he'd bite to mark her as his own when she came of age.

"Hey, yourself," she smiled, giggling when her panther purred loudly.

"She's wanting to run?" he asked, nipping her

earlobe. Evie bit her tongue, because all she wanted to do was tell him it wasn't the run she wanted. Her panther wanted him.

"I think so," she shrugged, turning in his arms. "I'm not going to run long tonight. I'm needed here to keep an eye on the house and the children. Talon wants Liberty to run with the pride tonight. My mother is taking the first shift with June."

"I can help you," he said, tightening his hold.

"You don't have to," she told him.

"But I want to." He nodded to someone behind her. "Here comes my brother. Let's get ready to go play, baby."

Talon cleared his throat as he reached the circle. The alpha sent out a calming presence through the pride, making everyone relax. Evie felt it and her shoulders slumped in response.

"My pride," Talon began. "We come to the circle on this Fall Equinox as a family. We have had fear and uncertainty in our lives, but I promise you that tonight will go on as usual. You are a superior race to our enemies, but I ask that if you are going to shift, you are to run with someone else. Do not go into the woods alone. If you see or hear anything that is out of the ordinary, you are to call out to me. I have Guardians in the woods and they will be close."

The pride nodded and swayed, feeling Talon's powers swirl around them. He was calling to their beasts, and Evie's was primed and ready to run.

"Go forth, my pride," he announced, holding his hands high. "Celebrate the change of season. You may shift now. Be safe, everyone."

Evie quickly removed her clothes, feeling her panther clawing to shed her human skin. The shift was quick; one second, she was a human, the next, she was a beautiful black panther.

The panther stretched lazily, raising her nose to the sky to sniff out familiar scents. Kye was close and his mating scent made the beast purr loudly. Others were taking off into the woods at full speed. She could hear the cackles and snarls from them as the sound echoed off the trees.

A nudge to her back leg had her turning to see Kye's panther standing there, an impatient look on his face. The male leaned in and nipped at her flank, sending her off at a fast trot. As soon as she reached the tree line, Evie ran.

It didn't take long before she found a tree to climb, digging her nails into the bark. She balanced on a tall limb, looking for Kye. He was below, waiting on her to come down. He huffed and scratched at the ground. He wanted to play.

Her panther squatted down close to the branch and gathered her strength in her hind legs, pushing off with so much force, she was able to get a head start on Kye. The beast snarled as he got closer, but still didn't catch up.

Her eyes took in every tree and shrub that lined

the path, always watching for enemies and other panthers. Scents of the other pride members were faint and she knew they were alone. The panther longed for the male she already considered hers.

Evie's human side understood. Kye was all she had ever wanted, and she really wished he'd make love to her before her birthday. The time was closing in, and she was excited and a little nervous about what that night would entail. Would he ravage her like some of the females had told her about? Or would he make love to her like he'd always promised?

And why in the hell was she acting like a dainty female? She was a badass female who fought with the Guardians. She should come on to him and be straight forward in her desires. Right? Maybe?

I have no idea how to seduce him.

With the push of her human thoughts, her beast stopped and fell to its belly, recessing back into her human skin. When Kye's panther rounded the large shrub on the trail and saw her laying on her back in human form, he snarled loudly before Kye's human form appeared.

"What's wrong? Are you hurt?" he worried as he fell to his knees at her side.

Evie took that moment to reach up and wrap her hand around the back of his neck, pulling him to her lips. "No, I want you to fuck me, Kye."

Her eyes flashed amber and a loud purring came

from her chest as his mating scent surrounded her. She glanced at his cock and it was long, thick, and very hard. She felt her response when an ache started between her legs. Her arousal wasn't missed by him. No, Kye's beast responded with his own animalistic sounds.

"You make it hard for me to be a gentleman," he warned as he took her lips.

"I don't want a gentleman," she groaned, reaching out with her foot to hook around his calf, twisting enough to lay him flat on his back. She threw her leg over his hips and sat across his erection. "I want it the way we were made to mate, Kye."

His canines thickened in his mouth as she pressed her lips to his. The sensation of his rough tongue against hers sent a wave of heat through her core. His nostrils flared as he nipped at her lips. The woods were silent around them as she tuned out everything except her male.

"Fuck, Evie," he panted. "You're killing me, baby."

"My beast needs you, and so do I," she hummed, feeling her wetness coat his cock where her pussy rested against his shaft. "Please, Kye."

"Fuck," he groaned, his eyes rolling into the back of his head. His body began to move, sliding his hardness between the lips of her sex, but he didn't breach her virginity. The skin of his erection was soft against her. A moan escaped her mouth and a purr rumbled in her chest. When Kye opened his eyes, they were completely amber and his scent strengthened, driving her insane with lust.

"Mount me," she breathed, her body tightened with anticipation.

"You are a temptress," he moaned, shifting his hips to force the roll, pinning Evie so she was flat on her back this time. His hand cupped her lower back where she'd had so much pain after her kidnapping. Even in the heat of the moment, he was careful. He didn't need to be soft with her. She was better and the pain was almost non-existent since she had started training.

"Are you going to give in?" she asked, her voice huskier than she meant it to be. She reached up and nipped at his muscular shoulder, making him shiver.

"No," he stated, his voice firm. "I've saved your body for our mating night. I want it to be perfect."

"Damn it," she cursed, a loud whoosh of air escaping her lips as she dropped her head to the hard ground.

"I know," he smirked, shifting his hips so his hardness would press into her leg. "Believe me. I don't know how I'm going to be able to walk home."

"Well, do you want to know what I'm going to do?" she teased, answering when he remained silent. "I'm going home to touch myself and think of you."

With that, she let her beast free, shifting beneath him. Kye jumped back, and Evie ran straight for her home to do exactly what she told him she was going to do.

Chapter Ten

"There will come a time when I am either no longer here, or I decide to retire as your alpha." Talon stood and looked out the window as he spoke, not looking at Kye as he proclaimed the future. "I need you to know what to do in case something were to happen to me."

"Where do we start?" Kye asked after swallowing a lump in his throat. He didn't even want to think about the possibility of his brother not being there.

"We need to talk about the legal part of this," Talon huffed as he turned around. "It's not something that a person wants to plan for, but it has to be done. Especially in the world we are living in now."

"What does all of that entail?"

"I'm having my final wishes drawn up," he frowned. "The two businesses I own will be split between you and Liberty. The home will go to her and Ember."

"Shit, Talon," Kye cringed. "I really don't want to think about that."

"It's a real possibility, Kye," Talon stated, his jaw tightening. His brother looked him dead in the eye, and he felt his alpha's push of power. "I need you to take care of Liberty and my daughter."

"Are you expecting something to happen?" Kye asked, looking at his brother as he began to pace.

"No." Talon shook his head. "I refuse to go out this soon. I've finally found my perfect half, and she's given me a child. My worry stems from all of these humans who have vowed to take us out because they are too scared to realize we want peace with them."

"We have security protocols in place that will keep you safe," Kye reminded him.

"Those are for my family. Not me," Talon said, fisting his hands at his sides.

"You are our leader, and anyone of us would die to protect you." Kye blew out a breath and continued, "Myself included."

"Let's not worry about that right now," Talon stated. Kye was sure that his brother felt his uncertainty and changed the subject. He was sure that once the paperwork arrived, they'd revisit that topic. "Come take a look at the program for the businesses."

For the next two hours, Kye learned the ins and outs of Shaw Security Specialists and Shaw Construction. Since the coming out and the problems with the *Community*, humans had been the only employees on the payroll. Winter was in charge of things behind the scenes, and kept a low profile within the companies, preferring to work from home so he wasn't in the offices. No one wanted their enemies anywhere near their human workers. It was just too dangerous if one of the other shifter species wanted revenge like the wolves had taken a few years ago.

"You are going to have to fight in the summer, you know that, right?" Talon raised a brow and waited for Kye to nod. "You are doing well training with Evie, but I need you to not train with the other Guardians. It's not allowed."

"I know this," Kye gritted out through his clenched teeth.

"Evie will need to train with Hope until you pass your Guardianship," Talon continued.

"She doesn't need to be training with any males after her birthday," he growled, feeling his panther raise his hackles. The thought of another male touching her after they'd mated sent his mind into a rage.

Talon sighed heavily and pinched the bridge of his nose. When he looked up, Kye knew his brother was going to ask the ultimate question. "Please tell me the two of you have discussed the possibility that you may not be fated to be mates?"

"We have," Kye snapped. "It doesn't matter. I love her, and she will be my mate."

"What if she touches another male and finds her true mate?" Talon asked as he leaned against his desk, folding his massive arms across his chest.

"I would let her go," Kye lied. There was no way he'd be able to handle her being with another male. It would kill him.

"You're lying to me," Talon growled. "Damn it, Kye. I've seen it before. The other party will go insane. Are you sure you can handle it if you are alpha and your female is destined to another?"

"I can't guarantee anything," Kye said truthfully. "What I can promise is that she is mine, I *know* it."

"You will need to make a decision if you touch and are not mates," Talon said. "For now, I need you to concentrate on learning the ropes to be my replacement. You will need to train with the other males who are wanting to fight in the summer. Malaki is giving the Guardians trouble with his attitude. This will be your first test. Go talk to the male and find out if he is ready to straighten up and be a functioning member of this pride."

"Fuck," Kye cursed, standing up to leave when his brother jutted his chin out toward the office door.

The situation with Malaki was strained, knowing his anger stemmed from his sister wanting to learn to protect herself. Just like Taze, and even himself, that male was going to have to warm up to the idea that the females were going to learn to fight regardless of what the males said.

The sheriff left his deputies at the gate to the

Shaw pride, driving up to the main house. There'd been no sign of anyone from the *Community* in town, and even though the relief from that felt good, Garrett knew it was probably a bad sign of things to come.

He parked his personal SUV around the back of the alpha's home, close to the back door. Guardians filed out the door as he opened up the back hatch, throwing aside the cloth tarp to reveal weapons.

"This is the first shipment," he said as Savage approached. The huge Guardian nodded and reached inside the back to grab a handful of assault rifles, handing them off to Noah, and then Ranger. The three males took a few trips to empty his personal vehicle. "I'll be back with more in a few days."

"Thank you," Talon said as he took the steps down from the porch. The alpha looked weathered and tired. The stress of the kidnappings of other shifters was wearing Talon down.

"Things are quiet..." He suddenly froze, his vision going white. He could hear the voices of the males around him, but he couldn't reply.

She was scared. Two men held her arms tightly as she was led into a hillside bunker. The walls were concrete and the lights that hung overhead were bright enough to hurt her eyes. She dug deep inside and cried for her alpha, but he never answered.

Talon! Help! Please!

Cries of others could be heard as they moved further into the corridors with unmarked doors. The males were supernaturally strong, but they were not of her kind. She tried to break free, but the guards only tightened their hold and rushed their steps. The cuffs on her wrists were unlike any that she'd used in training. Those she could break with her strength.

At the end of the hallway sat a metal door with a small window. When it opened, several men inside turned to look at her. Their faces were covered with masks like her healer wore when he was working on his patients.

"Ah, what do we have here?" one man asked as his eyes roamed her body.

"Female black panther," a guard said. "Careful, she's a fighter."

The guard removed her cuffs and pushed her into the arms of the other men, slamming the door behind her. She twisted and kicked out like she'd been trained, knocking one of them to the floor. The second, she punched in the jaw. Her fangs thickened and she pulled at her beast, but a familiar prick to her backside had her eyes going closed. She used all of her strength to fight the medicine. Another male shoved her against a wall, but she took that moment to bounce back and attack him. A fist caught her face, spinning the female to the side and directly into the arms of the male who looked at her like she was going to be his next conquest.

Talon!!!

"Garrett!" Talon snarled as the Watcher's vision fled.

"Where's Evie?" Garrett yelled, his heart thundering in his chest. That female couldn't be harmed again. If she was taken and killed, it would change the future of the shifters. It would destroy them.

"I'm right here," Evie called from the porch. She looked at the sheriff with an odd expression. "What's going on?"

"Inside! Inside now!" Garrett ordered, his eyes swinging to the alpha. "They're coming for her."

"What?" she gasped, her eyes flashing amber. "Who?"

"The *Community*," Garrett replied, taking long strides to reach the back porch. "Don't make me touch you, Evie. Get inside, now!"

Savage and Noah backed Evie into the house. Her icy blue eyes were wide with confusion. Ranger covered Talon as they made their way down the hallway to the security room that housed the safe room and all the weapons. Garrett was glad. They needed to keep the young female detained until they could sort through his vision.

"Tell me what you saw," Talon demanded as he whispered to Noah to go get his mate and child. He sent Savage to get Kye.

Garrett replayed the vision, word for word, as Evie sat in a rolling office chair. Ranger was squatted down next to her as if to give her comfort if she needed it, but Garrett knew the female wasn't going to back down, and he felt pride when she stood from her seat.

"They will not take me," she declared, her eyes flickering between icy blue and the amber of her beast. She rested the palm of her hand on the butt of the gun she carried with her whenever she was in human form. "I am never unarmed."

"My vision shows you going into an underground bunker. You have some type of cuffs on your wrists that you cannot break. The male guards are not human, nor are they shifters."

"Then what the fuck are they?" Ranger snarled.

"I have no idea," Garrett replied, pausing when the door to the room opened and Liberty came in, holding their daughter tight to her chest.

"What's going on?" she asked.

"Yeah, what the hell is going on?" Kye demanded as he barged in and went straight to Evie's side as Ranger stepped aside to give him room.

"Garrett had a vision of Evie being taken by the *Community*," Talon began. "They had her cuffed with restraints she couldn't break, and the guards are something unlike us. The place in his vision is an underground bunker. From what I can decipher from his vision, Evie cannot call out to me, because I am unable to answer."

"No," Liberty gasped, moving toward Talon's

side.

Kye nearly vibrated where he stood, his hand reaching for hers. Garrett saw the moment they squeezed hands as a sign of strength. He was glad that Kye hadn't lost his mind with the news. Evie was a strong female, and thankfully, the male that loved her saw that, as well.

"Fuck that nonsense," Liberty snarled. "She will not be taken by them."

"Agreed." Evie nodded to the alpha's mate.

Chapter Eleven

Evie swallowed hard. The news from the Watcher sent her worry into overdrive. She had to push away the flashbacks from her kidnapping to focus on the possibility it could happen again. Whatever he saw would come true, unless...

"I can change my fate, right?" she asked, squaring her shoulders.

"That's a possibility," Garrett said, nodding his head. "But we do not know what events take place for me to see you in that bunker. The path you are on now could be the one that saves you. If you choose to do something different, that could be the event that gets you caught. Does that make sense?"

"Yes," she nodded.

"You need to stay here," Kye said, wringing his hands as he began to pace. "It's too dangerous for you to be outside."

"Seriously?" she snapped. "Do you know what you are asking of me?"

"I'm asking you to stay somewhere safe," he replied.

"What if they come in here and take out the pride to get to me?" she growled. "I will not let that happen."

"The Guardians will be close," Talon promised,

wrapping an arm around his mate.

Evie watched the two as they snuggled close, holding Ember. The alpha's cub was fast asleep in Liberty's arms. At a year old, she hadn't even begun to live her life. What type of hell would Evie be bringing down on them if she was going to be the one targeted? She knew her pride was very protective of her ever since she'd survived her time with the wolves. There was no doubt in her mind that they'd fight to the death to protect her.

Obviously, the *Community* had been rounding up shifters from all over the world. The news stations reported daily on the takedowns of the hidden labs and jails that held the ones they'd caught. Deaths were nothing to them. They wanted more, and from the reports, they were finding them with ease.

"What is the government doing to protect us?"

"My deputies are posted at your gates." Garrett frowned. "What are you thinking?"

"I'm talking about the U.S government, the military. If they are so concerned with our safety, and the military are the ones shutting down these facilities, why haven't they sent more than just local deputies to protect us? Why do we only see them supposedly busting these hidden places, and during the removal of the deceased?"

"Because they are limited," Garrett answered, holding up his hand when she began to speak. "There is also a war on terrorism overseas. Our military is spread thin and local governments are trying to work with the National Guard to bust these facilities, but it's hard. They're very good at hiding."

Evie felt a tickle of awareness in her mind. Like she knew the answers to her own questions, but her brain just couldn't put her thoughts into words. When she looked up at Liberty, Evie knew she was on to something by the look of fear on the alpha's mate's face.

"Evie, no," Liberty growled, her eyes flashing amber.

"It needs to be done," she replied, standing her ground.

"What are you two talking about?" Talon ordered, pushing his powers out. Evie couldn't lie to him. His demands were law, and even if she wanted to lie to him, she couldn't. His powers were too strong.

"Find out where this bunker is… and send me in."

"*NO!*" The Guardians cursed so loudly, it hurt her ears. Kye growled low in his throat and walked right up to her. She had to look up into his amber eyes and what she saw there was fear.

"Are you fucking crazy?"

"Probably," she answered. "If you send me in, I may be the only one who can keep it together long enough to get information. You can plant a tracking device under my skin so I can be found. That way, you'll know where I am and how I got there. These people are obviously highly trained and have planned this for a very long time."

"So, you think the humans knew about us before the coming out?" Talon asked.

"It's been three years." She shrugged. "I honestly don't know, but I have a feeling that this could've been in the works before Kye and Ranger were seen shifting by the humans."

"Still doesn't matter," Kye barked. "You are *not* going in there voluntarily."

"Well, I sure as hell don't want them coming here," Evie replied, looking around the room at the family she had within the pride; blood or no blood. "It's too dangerous for the pride."

"It's more dangerous if you go in there," he paused, lowering his voice, "Your birthday is in three days, Evie. I don't want them touching you… hurting you."

Fuck! He was right. Her plan was solid, except for the pain of a male's touch if she and Kye were mated by that time.

"Then we don't touch each other until after this is over," she offered, wishing she hadn't.

Kye exploded with a round of curses, causing Talon to push his mate behind his back. The Guardians shouted out a warning to Kye when his hand wrapped around her upper arm. "We need to talk."

"You will let go of my arm first," she warned, her voice soft and even. She waited a few seconds more, but he didn't release her. "Two seconds, Kye, or I'll remove your hand myself."

"Son of a bitch!" Kye released her and stormed out of the office, slamming the door behind him. Evie released a breath and slumped into the closest chair.

"That didn't go over well," she whispered.

Kye stripped down and shifted as soon as he left the home. His claws scratched the wooden deck as he leapt from the porch, running across the backyard of his brother's home. He needed to be alone to process everything Evie had just said and done.

How could she offer herself up for another event that could be worse for her than the first?

An agonizing cry sounded from behind him, making his panther spin around to search for the sound that he knew came from Evie. The panther's heart galloped as he backtracked toward the house. She was calling out for him.

As he rounded a large tree, he saw her panther was running toward him. She slid in the wet leaves when she saw him standing there. Kye walked up to her and nipped at her ear, letting her panther and human side know he was not pleased with her decision. The male was angry at her for wanting to put herself in danger.

She whined and lowered herself to the ground, scooting on her belly until her head rested on his front paws. She whined again and looked up at him with the icy blue eyes of her human side. The panther shimmered and Evie's naked body appeared. She climbed to her knees and wrapped her arms around his panther's neck.

"Don't be angry with me," she whispered.

"I can't be angry with you," he sighed as he regained his human side.

"I have three days before my birthday," she began, reaching up to cup his face. Kye's panther purred from the softness of her hands. "If we touch and we are mates, I will still risk myself to keep this pride safe."

"We will protect you," he assured her.

"I cannot let Liberty or Ember be hurt," she growled. "What about Nova and Mary Grace? Their cubs, Landon and Atlas?"

"We have more ammo and guns now," he said, reaching up to hold her hand to his cheek when she started to pull away. "We are trained. Hell, *you* are trained, but I physically and mentally cannot let you leave this pride. It would be like throwing you to those wolves again."

"They will be coming for me at some point," she whimpered, showing her weak side. His girl had been so fucking strong and brave over the time she had been training, but this was setting her back and he refused to let that happen.

"And we will fight them when they come," he promised. "I'm not allowed to train at the Guardian's facility anymore, but I want you to be the one I train with on my own for the fights this summer. Evie, I need you strong, and I only trust myself to get you there. I promise you that I won't let them take you, but if they do, I want to have no doubt in my mind that you will be able to take them out on your own."

"Okay," she nodded, looking toward the ground. "Okay."

Chapter Twelve

Kye left his home to take off into the woods in his human form. His goal was to find Malaki and get him to see reason when it came to his sister, Calla. As much as he didn't want to deal with the male, he knew something had to be done. And since his brother had insisted he intervene, Kye obeyed.

It didn't take him long to reach the pond in the back of the property. He'd had a feeling this was where Malaki had been spending his time when he wasn't giving Calla a hard time about training.

"If you're here to talk, I don't want to hear what you have to say," Malaki barked when Kye approached.

"Then I'm here to train with you if you are wanting to try out for Guardianship in the summer," Kye stated. "I could really care less if you want that spot or not, but you will hear me out when it comes to your sister."

"I don't need you to tell me how to care for my blood," the male growled. Malaki stood and turned around, a look of hate marring his features. "You can go on back to your female."

"My female can take care of herself," Kye smirked. "Evie's a badass... just like Calla."

"You'd trust your female to be able to handle

another kidnapping?" Malaki chuffed.

"Yes," Kye answered.

"She's a *female*! They're too small to fight a male of our kind." Malaki walked toward Kye with his hands fisted at his sides. The male was too agitated to see reason, and that was just starting to piss Kye off.

"Listen," Kye began. "Let your sister learn to fight. It's that simple. Your anger at her is causing problems."

"Like what?"

"She's scared of you," Kye answered honestly.

"She shouldn't be," he huffed. "I'd never harm her... unlike you who will throw your fist at a female."

Kye'd had enough, launching himself at Malaki. One well-placed fist to the male's jaw sent Calla's brother to the ground, but he quickly regained his footing.

"I would never harm my female," Kye bellowed, his panther wanting blood. "You, on the other hand, need your ass kicked for being a pompous jackass."

Malaki charged Kye, grabbing him by the waist and knocking him to the ground. Kye rolled and came up over the male, hitting him with a right hook that caused blood to seep from the corner of his mouth.

"You need to train better," Kye growled, "because you suck at throwing a punch. Maybe Calla is better off protecting *you*."

"Fuck you, Kye," Malaki snarled, climbing to his feet. "I will never agree to be a Guardian to a pride that allows women to be harmed."

"We don't allow them to be harmed, you dumbass," Kye yelled. "They are learning self-defense, and if they want to help protect the pride, then so be it."

"I can't allow it," Malaki spat. "I'll get Calla and we will find another pride."

"She won't go," Kye argued. "You both belong here. After everything you've been through, our pride has taken you in as family, and this is how you repay us?"

"I owe you nothing!" the male shouted.

"No, you don't," Kye continued. "But you do owe it to your sister to let her live her life the way she wants to live it. If it's fighting alongside Guardians, then you need to accept that. Don't try and take her away, because all you'll do is destroy her."

"I don't need you to tell me what to do," Malaki snarled, shifting into his panther form and making his escape, deep into the woods.

Guardians lined the walls in Talon's office as he paced behind his desk. They were facing something that would test them and possibly destroy the pride in the very near future.

"The vision I saw was clear," Garrett explained. He was the only one Talon allowed in the meeting that wasn't a Guardian. Kye, his mate, Evie, and Hope were left out of this meeting for a reason. "They will be coming for Evie, and when they take her, it will be bad."

"How bad?" Taze asked, his eyes having changed to amber as soon as Evie's name was mentioned. The male had become close to the young female and thought of her as a baby sister. Hell, all of the Guardians had a special place in their hearts for that female.

"I saw guards taking her to a room full of scientists," he scowled. "The guards are something other than human. Why am I seeing them? I don't know, but in the vision, she knew they were something unlike anyone she'd seen before."

"I thought you could only see our human enemies?" Savage questioned.

"I have no idea." Garrett cursed, tossing his hands in the air. "There are no rule books to my mission here. For all I know, the gods may have now given me this ability for *anything* that comes your way."

"So, can we trust your vision?" Dane asked, fisting his hands at his sides. Talon sent out a calming presence to his Guardians when they all started to shift on their feet. He could feel their anger and aggravation.

"I'm trusting it," Garrett stated. "Evie is aware and has asked that we let her get caught so she can get inside this underground location to help us take them out. She wants us to imbed a tracker under her skin in case she is unable to call out for Talon."

The Guardians hollered and cursed at the sheriff's retelling of what the female had offered. Talon wasn't about to let her go in like that. As his brother said, it was too damn dangerous.

"Why wouldn't she be able to call out for Talon?" Taze asked.

"Because I would not be alive," Talon replied honestly.

"Fuck that!" Winter pushed away from the wall and approached the desk. "You will not be taken away from us."

"I have no plans on being taken out," Talon promised.

"Then I will come up with a new security plan," Winter vowed. "You and your family will not be alone until this is over."

"I am the alpha, and I will fight with my Guardians," Talon snarled, pushing out his powers so hard, the entire room fell to one knee. His anger was a thick blanket in the air that weighed down on everyone. "You all are to do your job of protecting the pride. If it is meant to be with your lives, then you fight to the death."

"Yes, alpha," they said in unison.

"Everyone in my pride is as special as my mate and cub," he said, looking around the room. His usual calm behavior had fled with the news of the possibility of Evie being taken again. "Evie is our main concern. I refuse to let that female be taken. We will change the course of the sheriff's vision."

"Yes, alpha," they repeated, still on bended knee.

"Winter," Talon barked, turning to look at the male. "Make your security plan with Noah and Dane. I want that information by tomorrow morning."

"I'll have it before midnight," Winter promised.

"Everyone is dismissed," the alpha snapped, taking a seat in his office chair. Everyone hurried out of the room. Even Garrett left without saying another word. As soon as the door closed, the silence surrounded him like a comforting blanket, allowing him to compose himself. His pride was in fear, and they had every right to be.

Their lives were at stake, and he was afraid someone was going to be lost to them before this was all over.

The sun was just starting to rise when a knock sounded on her window. Evie quickly opened the curtain to see who was there, but no one could be seen. She looked toward the road and could make out a silhouette of a male as he disappeared into the woods after shifting to his panther form. She frowned and looked down, seeing a letter on the windowsill. She raised the sash and grabbed the envelope that had been placed between the screen and glass, opening it with a smile on her face.

My dearest Evie,

I request your presence at my mother's home, our future home, at six p.m. tonight. A Guardian will escort you for safety.

Today, a series of gifts will be delivered to your door as mating gifts from me.

I know that you will be eager to come to me, but I ask that you take the morning and afternoon of your birthday to spend with your family, because the evening will belong to us.

I will be waiting for you.
Happy Birthday, baby.
Kye

Evie closed the letter and pressed it to her chest. After they'd come to an understanding about her desire to turn herself over to the *Community* and the danger behind it, Kye had been her rock, training her in the backyard of his mother's old home for the past three days. She knew the possibility of her being taken was imminent, and she wanted to put him at ease by agreeing not to turn herself over willingly.

Winter had made a solid security plan, but Evie believed the Watcher and his vision. It was only a matter of time before she was captured.

"Evie!" her mother called from the front room.

She set the letter aside and ran down the hallway. Her mother stood at the door to their home and pointed to the porch. "You have a delivery."

There was a small box wrapped in brown paper, a blue ribbon tied around it with a small bow on top. Evie took it to her room and climbed onto her bed. She held it in her hands as she felt tears well up in her eyes.

Pulling on the ribbon released the package, and she tore at the paper carefully. The box beneath was the same color as the ribbon. She took a deep breath before opening the lid and pulling back the tissue paper.

Evie reached inside and her fingers touched a thin metal band. She pinched it carefully, pulling it from the box. With a gasp, she held up the bracelet, allowing the morning sun to dance across two beautiful topaz stones that were connected to an infinity symbol. The band was made of white gold, and her hands shook as she tried to attach it to her wrist. It took a few tries, and she almost called her mother to come help, but she finally worked the clasps to get it connected. She twisted her hand, testing the weight and fit, realizing Kye had known exactly what size she needed. Picking at the remaining tissue paper, she found a note at the bottom of the box.

This gift is for the first time I truly saw you and realized you were going to be mine forever.

It was another two hours before the next box arrived much like the first, but this time, the box was bigger.

Inside, Evie found a new pair of gloves for her training. They were all black and small enough for her hands. The ones she'd been using were an unused pair that Ranger had found in a box toward the back of a storage closet when she'd begun training over a year ago.

Inside was another note:

This gift is for your strength and my acceptance of the woman you have become.

She wiped away a tear of happiness and tried on the gloves after removing the bracelet. They fit her perfectly and she would always cherish them, just as she would any gift Kye bestowed upon her. She placed them on her dresser and walked out to show her mom his first gift.

"Oh, Evie," Marie smiled, touching the side of Evie's face. "You are one lucky female."

"I am," Evie agreed.

"When is he going to come over?" her mother asked.

"He's sending a Guardian to collect me at six," she blushed. "I don't even know what to wear or take with me. What if I screw this up? I don't want to make a fool of myself."

"You could never do that." Marie chuckled when Evie frowned. "He loves you, dear. Just be yourself."

"I'm nervous and ready," she sighed. "It's going to be a long day."

"How about I make you something to eat?" her mother offered.

"Thank you," she replied, following her mother into the kitchen.

She sat at the table and watched her mother work, looking like she was meant to be there. The one thing about Marie Sawyer, she loved caring for everyone in the pride. She took her duties in the kitchen like she'd been handed a special order from the alpha himself. Evie had never heard her mother complain about any aspect of her life.

"Mother?" Evie cleared her throat. "May I ask you a question?"

"Of course you can, my sweet girl." Marie turned with a smile, but it died on her lips when she saw Evie's look of sadness.

"What if we touch tonight and are not mates?" Evie asked, chewing on her bottom lip.

"Do you love him?" Marie asked, setting a plate in front of her.

"More than my own life," Evie vowed.

"You answered your own question, daughter." Marie smiled and ran an old weathered hand over her head.

"We've talked about it," she said sadly. "We will marry and live as a mated couple, but what if he finds the woman he is fated to be with?"

"Then there is a male out there for you, too," Marie offered. Evie knew her mother wasn't sugar-coating anything, and while she appreciated it, the thought of Kye being with another female had her panther clawing to get out so it could find her and kill her.

"Your beast doesn't like that idea, huh?" Marie raised a brow.

"No, she doesn't," Evie frowned.

Chapter Thirteen

"Stop pacing," Talon chuckled, watching his little brother wear a hole in the rug that sat in front of his desk. Kye had been there for the last hour, trying to pay attention to what Talon had to say, but it was pointless. Kye was too busy thinking about his mating night with Evie.

"I can't," Kye grumbled, wiping his brow. "I'm nervous."

"Haven't you two had sex yet?" Talon asked, sensing his brother's nervousness was about the entire process.

"No," Kye blurted. "And I'm definitely not talking to you about that."

"I don't want to talk to you about that either, but as your alpha…" Talon began, but was cut off when Kye narrowed his eyes.

"Please don't," Kye responded. "I need my brother right now. Not my leader."

"Kye," Talon sighed and stood up so he could walk around his desk. He reached out and wrapped his arm around Kye's shoulder, pulling him in for an awkward brotherly hug. "Your nature will guide you. This is the only thing I can promise you about your mating."

"Let's change the subject, or else I'll break my

rule of not seeing her until this evening," Kye said, pulling away.

"Okay," Talon nodded. "Have you talked to Malaki?"

"Yeah, about that," Kye flinched. "He's not budging on his total assholiness."

"What happened?"

Talon listened as Kye replayed the events of his talk with the male. It sounded to Talon like Malaki's maturity wasn't settling well, and he was making some rash decisions. He'd have to have a meeting with Calla and Malaki together to get a clear picture of what was going on with them and their plans for the future.

"I'll take care of them from here on out," Talon said. "I'm so glad you're not being a jerk."

"I have too much to worry about right now," Kye replied. "I can't afford to be out of my right mind around Evie."

"Well done, brother," Talon said with pride.

"When do I need to be here tomorrow?"

"Take the next few days off," Talon smirked. "Your panther is going to demand you stay with your mate."

"Okay," Kye blushed. "I need to go. I have one last gift to send to Evie before dark."

"Go, be with your mate," Talon urged, shooing Kye toward the door.

As soon as his brother left the room, Liberty

appeared at the door. His mate was smiling from ear to ear. "Have they touched yet?"

"No," Talon chuckled. "He's making her wait until this evening. At least he's courting her the old way."

"The old way?" Liberty frowned. "What's that?"

"Ancient times were… different," he began, pausing to open his arms so Liberty would come to him. When she snuggled against his chest, he kissed the top of her head and continued. "Males would send gifts to the women they wanted to touch to see if they were mates. The women would then be escorted to the male's home he'd built for them. The night would be their official first touch, then they wouldn't come out until their beasts were fully sated."

"You didn't send me gifts," she huffed, jokingly nudging him in the side.

"I didn't court you," he reminded her. "We touched by accident, and then I had to convince you that you were mine."

"I did play hard to catch, didn't I?" Liberty chuckled and moved away, but not far. "I'm glad I finally gave in to your charms."

"My charms?" he teased, raising a brow. "If I remember correctly, you gave in when my tongue brought you to orgasm."

"Well, that too," she blushed. "Think maybe you can charm me some more tonight?"

"How about we start right now?" He scooped her

up in his arms and kissed her into silence as he left the office, hurrying toward their bedroom upstairs.

Dane entered the bar, his eyes immediately falling on Cole and Olivia talking at the bar top. Both of them looked up when he approached. The tiny, blonde female smiled warmly at him and backed away.

"You don't have to leave on my account," he teased, sealing that with a wink.

"Don't flatter yourself," she rolled her eyes, "I have work to do."

With that smartass comment, she turned on her heel and walked toward the kitchen. When Dane's eyes landed on Cole, the bartender chuckled softly and reached for a bar towel to dry a glass.

"What'll it be today?"

"Just a beer," Dane said, looking at the clock on the wall. "It's time to open. Want me to turn the sign?"

"Please," Cole replied.

As soon as Dane stood up, he felt the human male's gaze on his back, and for some reason, his panther preened from the attention. He'd been working at the bar as security for the past several weeks. With Liberty now working from home and staying out of the reach of the *Community*, Dane was tasked with keeping her business from being infiltrated by the people who wanted to take out the shifters.

He flipped the sign and turned away from the door, only to spot that new waitress, Olivia. She was gathering an order pad from behind the bar and tucking into the black apron all the waitresses wore with the bar's logo on it. Her gaze flickered to Cole, looking away when the male turned toward her. When she did, her eyes landed on him. He held her stare for a moment before giving her a wink and walking toward the bar to pick up his beer.

"It's Tuesday," Cole said, clicking the remote to turn on the televisions over the bar. "It'll be quiet in here most of the day."

"Let's hope it stays that way," Dane replied, taking a seat.

"So, explain to me what exactly is going on with the *Community*," Olivia inquired, taking a seat next to Dane. He automatically shifted to the right to keep his distance. She blushed and whispered, "Sorry."

"So, I guess Liberty told you about us?" Dane asked, raising a curious brow as he moved to stand on the other side of the barstool.

"She asked me to keep a healthy distance from y'all," she said with a shrug. "She said the shifters didn't like the contact."

"That's all she said?" Dane asked.

"Yep," Olivia said with a little pop to the end of her word. "I respect that, and I promised the boss lady I'd adhere to the rules."

"Truth is," Dane started, then smiled. "We don't mind the touching. It's just that we find our mates that way. One touch and that's all we need to go into a mating... well, frenzy."

"Oh," she squeaked as she blushed.

"Yeah, we tend to keep our distance until we find someone who we are interested in." He shrugged and took a long pull off of his beer, watching her eyes darken. "If we feel a good connection to them, there will be touching involved... lots of touching."

"I see." She nodded and grabbed a bar towel that'd been hanging from her tied apron strings. "I need to go wipe down some tables."

Dane watched Olivia walk away, making note of how her hips swung seductively. It wasn't like she was trying, either. He'd seen those kinds of women more than enough in the bar. You always knew who the ones were that were only there to pick up a shifter. What did Nova call them? Oh, yeah... pride whores.

Chapter Fourteen

I give this ring to you as a mating gift from me. Our vows will be said at the Winter Solstice, but until then, take this as a symbol of our bond.

Evie slid the silver band onto her left ring finger. It fit snug against her skin and she tested the weight, realizing Kye had found her a ring she could still wear if she ever had the need to fight. It wouldn't hinder her in any way.

A soft knock sounded on the front door, and her mother began to tear up. Her father stood tall and squeezed Evie's hand before walking to the door. Noah, Kye's brother, was standing there on the porch. His smile was bright as he nodded toward her father.

"Mr. Sawyer," Noah began, "I am here as a Guardian of the Shaw pride to safely escort your daughter to meet with her destined mate on the eve of her twentieth birthday. Do you give permission for your daughter's hand to be sought by Kye Shaw?"

"I do," her father said, moving aside so Evie could step over the threshold. It was an ancient ritual, one not often practiced anymore, but Evie didn't mind. Kye had been a little old fashioned in his way of thinking up until a year or so ago when she began learning how to fight. The thought of him planning everything for their evening sent a thrill through her veins.

It was time.

Her mother handed her a backpack and kissed her cheek, whispering, "Call me in a few days."

Evie nodded and followed Noah as he began to walk. The road up to the home she'd share with Kye was paved with worry, nervousness, and excitement. There was also a sadness that hung over her, and Noah as well, the closer they got to the house where his mother had once lived.

"You don't have to walk me the entire way," she whispered, knowing he could hear her with his enhanced hearing. Noah had the hardest time with the death of their mother, resorting to drinking heavily to numb the pain. He'd been doing better since the alpha had stepped in, but Evie could tell that he still mourned the loss.

"No," Noah shook his head. "I'm okay. This is a special night, and I'm happy for you and my brother."

"Okay, thank you," she replied, and kept walking.

The cabin lights were on. A soft yellow light shone from the window in the living room. The porch light was on over the door, and she released a breath as she climbed the steps behind Noah. He knocked on the door and stepped aside.

Kye opened the door, and the first thing she

noticed was that he was wearing denim jeans and a baby blue, button-down shirt that she loved. He didn't look at her right away, and she knew this was tradition.

"Kye Shaw," Noah smiled. "I have escorted your fated mate, Evie Sawyer, to you as you have requested."

"Thank you." Kye nodded, looking at her for the first time.

She'd fretted all day about what to wear. Evie wasn't one for frilly dresses or girly things. Her mother had eventually stepped in and told her to wear whatever she wanted. There was no dress code for this sort of thing. Evie had chuckled and thought that it really didn't matter about the clothes toward the end of the night, either. After her mother's pep talk, she'd decided on jeans and a soft beige sweater.

"Hey, baby," Kye greeted, stepping back into the house so she could pass without being touched. She really just wanted to say fuck tradition and get on with it, but she'd wait because it was important to him.

"Hey."

Evie looked around and saw that Kye had placed small candles sporadically throughout the living room. Several were placed on the mantel above the fireplace. Two small glass holders were on the coffee table.

"Come," he said, holding his hand out toward the

kitchen, "I've made you dinner."

"Thank you," she replied, walking into the kitchen. The table was set for two. Tall pillar candles were lit on the centerpiece made of fall leaves and vines.

Kye took his seat after pulling out her chair. He waited until she was seated to hand her plates of food and bowls of vegetables. He'd made grilled chicken and mashed potatoes. There was a warm loaf of bread in a basket, wrapped in a red cloth.

"Thank you for my gifts," she said, holding out her left hand to show him the bracelet and ring. She kept her new gloves in her backpack, because she wanted to make sure she had them for the next time they sparred.

"You're welcome."

Kye nodded and tucked into his food. She was nervous, but ate as much as she could. The thought of food was making her ill, but her panther pushed her to eat. Her strength was important, and the animal inside her knew they would be in for a workout later. Again, she blushed from her thoughts.

"Relax on the couch while I clean up," Kye said as he picked up their plates.

Evie took a seat, but she couldn't relax. All she could think about was when they'd touch. She wiped her hands on her jeans and wondered how he planned on doing it. Would he just come over and kiss her? Did he have some ritual he wanted to attempt for the contact?

"Stop worrying," Kye said, standing in the doorway that led to the living room from the kitchen.

"I don't know what to do," she admitted, biting her bottom lip when she noticed his eyes were throwing amber sparks.

"Stand up," he ordered, moving around the table that sat in front of the couch. "We can either do it here, or go to my room upstairs."

"Here," she blurted, feeling heat creep up her neck. "Just do it, Kye. I've waited long enough."

"If you're sure," he grinned, moving to stand in front of her.

"I am," she whispered, looking up into his eyes. He was so close, she could feel the warmth coming off of his body.

"I'm going to kiss you now," he warned as his hands raised to cup her face.

Evie closed her eyes in anticipation. This was it... the night they'd been waiting to arrive for over three years. They didn't have to live separately anymore, or go by the terms of boyfriend and girlfriend. It was time to be mates, forever.

Kye cupped her face and immediately pressed his lips to her, starting slow. The passion of the kiss heated, coiling tightly around her body. His tongue was rough, but it didn't matter because so was hers. Heat swirled between them from the dire need for each other, but nothing happened.

The spark wasn't there.

The overwhelming urge to mate was nonexistent.

"*No*," they both gasped.

Evie's birthday had come to an end… and Kye was not her mate.

The healer put away supplies as he watched the local news. The breaking story was yet another hidden facility used by the *Community* being busted and the people inside were arrested.

A source close to the National Guard has confirmed that they have now started finding shifters in other forms than human. This facility alone has been found with the bodies of wolves, black panthers, and brown bears. It is assumed, but not proven, the animals are part human. An autopsy has been ordered on the remains.

"Fuck," Harold cursed, his heart aching for the ones who were lost.

How many more hidden facilities were there? So far, the count was five, but he was sure there were more. According to the sheriff, there was one that might possibly take Evie, and the Shaw pride had vowed to keep her safe until the danger was over.

Harold was sure that the sheriff's vision was indeed going to come true. The Watcher had abilities beyond simple supernatural enhancements. They'd been searching histories and mythologies to find out what type of other beings had been seen in his vision of them taking Evie to the scientists, and so far, had come up with two possibilities: vampires or aliens.

Vampires were few and far between. They kept so well hidden, Harold hadn't seen one since he had been a young cub. Thankfully, their kind were not enemies. As far as the aliens, the healer had to laugh. It wasn't a possibility. The human government had too many technologies in place for an extraterrestrial being to be able to slip past to infiltrate the Earth, let alone work for a cult such as the *Community*.

A knock on the door brought him out of his thoughts. He set aside a box of gloves and opened the door to find Talon standing there with his wife's hand held tightly in his. The overwhelming calm that hit him square in the chest had the healer smiling. Liberty's scent was strong, and the alpha's concern was thick in the air.

"So, looks like we have another cub on the way." Harold grinned, hiding the worry over another innocent being brought into the world they lived in that was no longer safe.

Chapter Fifteen

"This means nothing," Kye panicked. "You are mine and I am yours, forever, Evie. This is something I promise you."

"I know," she cried, a soft hiccup signaling her strength as she tried to hold the tears back.

"I love you," Kye promised, cupping her face. He said a silent prayer that the spark would come at any moment, but the longer they touched, nothing happened.

"I've loved you for what seems like forever, Kye," she vowed. "Please, tell me what we do now?"

"We continue," he whispered, taking her lips for a heated kiss.

His body relaxed when her arms came up to wrap around his neck. The panther inside him cried when he opened his eyes to see the wetness on her cheekbones. With the hands that still held her face tenderly, Kye used his thumbs to wipe away the evidence of her sadness. Evie's eyes opened and her panther was present by the amber hue to her eyes.

"You are my mate," he vowed through his thickening canines. It didn't matter that fate had dealt them the wrong hand. Kye was going to mark her as his own. "I will mark you as such tonight, baby."

"But it will heal," she reminded him. The bite of

unmated couples wouldn't scar over, and he knew that.

"It doesn't matter," Kye stated, holding her close as he scooped her up into his arms. "You are my mate regardless of what our nature says."

Kye carried her to the bedroom, kicking the door closed. He didn't speak as he laid her out on the bed. The nervousness from earlier was gone. His brother was right, in a sense. Although the need to frantically mate Evie wasn't there, his beast knew exactly what to do.

He removed his shirt and climbed in the bed to lay next to her. Evie rolled on her side to meet him, taking his lips in a desperate attempt to seal their fate. As soon as the scent of her desire reached him, his cock had hardened almost to the point of pain and his need for her was unexplainable.

His claw unleashed and hooked in the top of her shirt, tearing the material right down the center. Her bra was sliced, and within seconds, her breasts were bared to him. Evie cursed as his tongue laid a path over her hardened nipple.

"Kye," she breathed, melding her body closer to his.

"Evie," he replied, reaching for the fly of his jeans. The moment his cock sprang free, Evie's hands wrapped around the hardness. "Fuck."

"Mmhmm," she hummed as he reached out to remove the remainder of her clothes.

"Beautiful," he growled as his hands grabbed at her waist. He just wanted to feel her skin beneath his fingertips, memorizing everything about her.

"Touch me, please," she panted.

Kye covered her body with his own, letting his fingers trail down to her sex. Evie raised her hips automatically when he touched her core. She was wet for him, and it took all of his restraint to keep from thrusting his cock into her tightness.

Their kisses were frantic as he slid a finger inside her, working it in and out. She was still a virgin, and he wanted to make the night perfect. The last thing he intended to do was hurt her.

Evie's hand slid between them as she began to circle her clit, moaning louder as her body opened up to accept his touches. He watched for signs of discomfort, and when he found none, he added another finger to work her closer to orgasm.

"Kye...I need you inside me, please," she begged, tightening her hold around his shoulders. "Mate me like we are destined."

"Roll over, baby," he ordered, moving so she could scramble into position. "Tell me if I hurt you."

Kye leaned over her body, taking his aching cock and guiding it to her entrance. As soon as her resistance broke, Kye seated himself inside, barely moving so she wouldn't cry out. What he didn't expect was for his panther to push to the point of his face shifting, his canines elongating to sharp points.

The animalistic growl that came from his throat caused Evie to look over her shoulder.

The moment their eyes locked on one another, he saw that her beast was there, sitting just under her skin. She bucked against him and snarled, "Bite me, damn it."

Kye made a fist in the back of her hair, pulling her upright. He licked a path over the spot where her neck met her shoulder, then struck hard. Evie cried out, her body convulsing with her climax. She was paralyzed against his punishing thrusts. Blood seeped into his mouth as she shivered. He reluctantly released her, swiping his tongue over her mark.

When she was free, Evie pushed back, dislodging him from her sex. Kye smiled when she pushed him over to his back, taking his cock back inside her body. His mate took no time in striking the spot on his shoulder, claiming him for her own. Her bite sent a shockwave down to his cock, and he cursed in pleasure as he emptied inside her. A sadness squeezed at his heart, knowing his seed would never settle in her womb.

Evie panted as she snuggled her body into his embrace. The rise and fall of their chests kept them from talking for a few minutes. Kye stroked her long blonde hair, pulling it away from the mark he'd made. The pain in his chest caused his panther to whine when he watched the area heal over as if it was nothing more than a scratch.

"It's gone, isn't it?" she mumbled, nuzzling her nose against his chest.

"Yes, baby," he breathed. "We are not going to let this change things."

"I know," she replied, raising her head. She eyed the spot on his neck and closed her eyes when she saw that his mark had faded as well. A tear slid down her cheek, but she wiped it away before he had the chance to do it for her.

"No little bastard children for you."

"I hate these fucking cats."

"Go ahead and shift with that collar on, you'll be doing your pride a favor. They won't care for you anymore if you can't breed."

"No male will want a female who can't give him babes."

"Sedate her."

A scream bubbled out of her throat as she came awake, panting when she scrambled from the bed. There was a body beside her, touching her, and she didn't know who it was. When the male moved, she screamed.

"Evie!" Kye called out as she dropped to her knees, lowering her head to the ground. She didn't cry, nor did she speak as Kye wrapped his large body around hers, holding her as tight as he could. "It's going to be okay. It's over."

"It's not going to be okay," she growled, slamming her fists against the ground. "None of this is going to be okay until it's finally over, Kye!"

Evie didn't know how long he just sat there, holding her on the floor, but at some point, Kye scooped her up and brought her back to the bed, pulling the sheet up over their bodies. He rolled her over so he could spoon up against her back. She didn't miss the gentle placement of his hand over her womb.

"I need to shower." Evie couldn't stay in that bed. She had to get away from him. At that moment, she couldn't be around him.

"Let me..." he began, but she cut him off when she frantically pushed at his hands and slid from the bed.

"I need a moment to myself, please," Evie said, backing away from the bed.

Chapter Sixteen

Talon took a deep breath as he arrived at the Morgan clan's property. The bears were a fickle bunch. They hated visitors, and the alliance they shared was only connected by a small thread.

"What are you doing here, Talon?" Drake Morgan growled as he stepped off the rustic porch of his old home. His brother Rex exited with a shotgun in hand. Gunner appeared from around the side of the house, setting something down behind a bush.

"Have you been watching the news?" Talon inquired, keeping his hands in sight. The bears were easy to agitate and could attack you without warning. Just like the natural bears in the wild, you didn't mistake their slow movements for weakness.

"We don't pay attention to humans or their television," Drake grunted. "Don't care for them much."

"There has been a hate group calling themselves the *Community*, and they have been rounding up shifters. Reports have stated they are holding shifters for the sake of research. It has come to our attention that they've gotten their hands on wolves, panthers, and bears. I'm here to offer assistance in security if you are of need."

"We are not known in this area." Drake raised a brow. "I think we can cover ourselves if the need arises." The male bear's eyes darkened and his upper lip raised at the corner, showing off long, thick fangs.

"I'm just here to give you information." Talon raised his hands in the air slowly, backing toward his truck. "The local sheriff has been gathering information. These places being raided are housing several of our kind. There have not been any found alive at this point."

"Noted," Drake nodded, jutting his chin out in dismissal. "I'll take care of my own, thank you."

"You know where to find me," Talon offered in parting. He slipped inside his truck and left as quickly as he had arrived.

Shifters had been around for thousands of years, but they'd kept hidden. Talon only knew of a few prides outside of his own, and only one bear clan; that being the Morgan's. Word over the years had estimated that there were packs of wolves, prides of panthers, and clans of bears spread out in rural areas all over the United States. How were they being found?

Raindrops scattered across the windshield as he drove away. A sense of dread came over him and he locked down the worry for their future. The darkening sky felt like an omen as he turned into the driveway to the pride's land. He nodded toward Savage and one of the sheriff's deputies.

When he arrived at his home, Talon headed directly to his office, wishing he could just go to his room and rest with his mate. She'd been tired that morning after realizing she was now carrying their second cub. Talon smiled widely with pride at knowing he'd made another child with his beloved mate, refusing to think about what the future held for his cherished offspring.

"Evie?" Talon questioned as he opened the door to his office. The young female was sitting patiently in the chair by his desk. "What can I do for you?"

"I need to talk to you, alpha." Evie looked up with sparking amber eyes. "This is important, and I need you to hear me out."

"Okay," Talon said, walking around to take a seat at his desk. "What is it?"

"Your brother and I are not fated mates." She released a heavy sigh. "I've thought about this long and hard. I want you to allow me to be caught by the *Community* so I can get in there to bring them down."

"No," he barked, slashing his hand through the air. There was no way he would put a female in that much danger on purpose. Allowing Evie to be captured again was never going to happen on his watch. "I will not let you be taken again."

"It has been seen that I will be there anyway," she argued. "I am strong enough to keep myself from being harmed, Talon. The fact that your brother and I did not have the spark when we touched will make it easier for me to go inside this facility the Watcher has seen in his vision. A male's touch will not hurt me."

"Have you spoken to Kye about this?"

"No," she stated, narrowing her eyes. "I love him, but he does not rule my actions. This is my decision."

"It goes against everything I stand for to let you, or any of my pride for that matter, be kidnapped and taken to a facility where they could be studied like lab rats."

"Have the healer imbed a tracker under my skin," she said. "Even if I am comatose, you can find me."

"Do you honestly think you can handle another kidnapping?" Talon asked, knowing he was being crude, but the female was stronger now and needed to know what she was asking for. "They could hurt you again, maybe even violate you, Evie. Think about it."

"Talon," she growled, gritting her teeth. "I have nothing left to lose. The wolves have made me infertile, Kye is not my fated mate, and the only thing I have left is my knowledge and training. This has to stop somewhere, and I am volunteering to be the one to set that in motion."

"No," Talon repeated. "I'm not going to allow that."

"But you know it's going to happen," Evie yelled. "The Watcher saw it!"

"As your alpha, Evie, do not make me order you to stand down," Talon warned. "We will keep you safe, and we will find another way to stop the *Community*."

"Then have Harold imbed the tracker in me anyway," she begged. "They're coming for me, and when they do, I want to be prepared."

"They won't get to you," Talon snarled.

"They will, alpha," Evie said as she stood from her seat. "And when they do, I will go with them willingly."

The female stormed out of the room, leaving the door to his office wide open. Talon knew she was right, but he wasn't going to allow her to just walk into their hands. If there was anything an alpha could do to get himself killed by his pride, it was to willfully hand over a female to an enemy. No matter the circumstances.

Talon picked up the phone and dialed the healer. Harold answered on the second ring. "Alpha? Is everything okay with your mate?"

"Yes, she is fine," Talon replied, pinching the bridge of his nose. "I need you to get with Storm and Dane. We need you to imbed a tracker in Evie."

Storm Cooper held the tiny disk in the palm of his hand. The blonde Guardian looked apprehensive, but set the thing on a tray next to the healer. Evie nodded and lay back on the table. Booth sat in a chair on the other side of her head, holding his phone carefully as he entered information into an app he'd use to track her whereabouts.

"Before we start," Harold said, pulling the paper mask up over his mouth. "The site will be red and irritated for a few hours. Keep the bandage on it until morning. You should be healed by then."

"Okay," she sighed, holding her arm out to the side. The plan was to put it inside the top part of her arm. The disk was so small, only a tiny incision would be needed.

"Have you told your mate?" Harold asked, raising a brow at her as he sat back on his stool.

"I guess you all should know," Evie sighed heavily, "Kye and I are not fated mates."

"I'm so sorry," Harold said, reaching over to squeeze her hand. Booth stood at the doorway with an equally sad expression.

"No need to be sorry." Evie shook her head. "This problem with the *Community* and the vision the Watcher had needs to be dealt with before I can move on with him."

"No, this doesn't," Booth growled. "The Watcher could be wrong, Evie."

"He's not," she replied, looking over at the healer. She just wanted to get this over with so she could go on about her night. "Please do it, Harold."

The healer reached for a packet of iodine to clean

the area he was going to cut open for the disk. Evie had told him there was no need to numb the area. The incision wasn't going to be that painful. At least, that was what she'd understood.

"I'm going to make the incision," Harold said aloud. Evie sucked in a breath through her clenched teeth when the cold blade cut her skin. She looked toward Booth instead of the healer, hoping she was making the right decision.

"The disk is going in," the healer mumbled. Evie felt the pressure, but there was no more pain as he finished up, wiping down her arm with something cold and wet. A second or two later, he placed the bandage over the site and removed his gloves. "It's done."

"Thank you." She smiled, sitting up carefully. She looked at her arm and flexed it, realizing the disk wasn't going to be felt by her or hinder her in anyway. "If someone touches it, will they know?"

"No," Harold stated. "It's in there pretty deep."

"Good," she said, looking toward the Guardian Storm. "Is it working?"

Storm punched a few buttons on his phone and waited several seconds for the program to load. They'd explained some of it to Evie earlier in the day. The tracker worked with a satellite signal, and with the program the Guardians used, she'd be able to be found anywhere in the world.

The door to the healer's home and office burst

open, causing Evie to reach for her weapon and aim it in the direction of the commotion. Booth and Storm immediately went into defensive mode. Harold put his body as close to hers as possible, only leaving enough room for her to be able to discharge her weapon if needed and growled low in his throat. A male came around the corner at top speed, but Booth grabbed him, slamming the intruder against the wall.

"Kye!" Evie roared, holstering her gun. Booth's eyes glowed bright with his beast on a hair trigger. "What are you doing?"

"I came to ask you the same thing," Kye snarled, pushing at the Guardian who still had him pinned.

"It's none of your business," she replied, feeling her panther pace in her mind.

"The fuck it isn't," he spat, pushing Booth away so he could come to her side. Harold moved out of the way, and she gasped when Kye grabbed her wrist and lifted her arm. "They put a tracker in you?"

"Yes," she admitted, using her free hand to cup his cheek, praying her touch would calm him. "It needed to be done, Kye. The *Community* is coming for me, and I asked them to do it."

"You are not leaving me!" Kye bellowed, his voice so loud, it shook a few items on the tray next to the table.

"I'm going to do what needs to be done to stop them," she told him, resigned. "The sheriff saw it, Kye. My time here is short, and I refuse to let others be hurt if I can get in there to signal to our Guardians where this place is so we can shut it down for good."

"No," he cried, dropping her hand and using both of his to cup her face tenderly. "Evie, I cannot let this happen. You've been through so much."

"I'm stronger now," she said, straightening her spine.

"No one is that strong," he whispered. Evie looked around his shoulders to see Booth and the healer standing guard not far from Kye as if they were prepared to physically remove him if he got out of hand.

"Can I leave now?" she asked Harold.

"Yes, remember to keep the bandage on until tomorrow morning."

On her nod, the two males exited the room. Evie didn't speak to Kye as she grabbed her things and walked out of the healer's home. When she reached the road, she sighed and turned toward him. "Let's go home."

Chapter Seventeen

As soon as the door closed, Kye picked Evie up and wrapped her legs around his waist. The scent of the small amount of her blood from the incision sent his panther into a snarling frenzy. He was born a predator, and blood was something that was easy to detect. The fact that the coppery scent belonged to his female made his panther uneasy, thinking she was hurt.

"I'm so angry with you right now," he snarled, tightening his hold.

"Everyone needs to realize I might be abducted again," she said softly, resting her forehead on the top of his shoulder. Kye walked over to the couch and sat down, but didn't release her. "I took it upon myself to go to Talon and offer to give myself to the *Community*, but he denied me."

"Damn right, he should've denied you," Kye barked.

"Thankfully, after I left his office, the alpha agreed to let me be implanted with a tracking device so I could be found if the Watcher's vision comes true."

"Are you not scared?" he asked, needing to get inside of her mind. Evie was strong; so much stronger than she was three years ago, but this way of thinking was almost suicidal.

They wanted to hurt her… to make her infertile. Too weak to fight…

"I'm terrified," she admitted.

"If, and I mean *if*, they get you, I promise to come for you," Kye vowed. "And I will kill them with my bare hands."

"I know you and the pride will keep me safe," Evie said, stroking the side of his face. "I'm stronger than before, and I will fight them this time."

Kye closed his eyes, wishing the magic that picked their mates would work for him and Evie. At that moment, he'd give anything to have her as his destined mate so he could use that to remind her that giving herself up would be painful. Maybe she'd hesitate with her plans, but in all reality, Kye knew she would do it regardless.

"Until we know if the sheriff's vision will come true or not, I want you to train every single day, twice a day if you can."

"I agree," she whispered, taking his lips.

Kye relished in her taste and the scent of her desire. He turned to the side and laid her against the couch cushions, hovering over her body.

"Make love to me, Kye," she whispered.

"We have twenty-five men in place to take down the Shaw pride," a voice crackled over the cell phone that sat on the desk on speakerphone. The *Community* had put out orders for the takedown of this pride's leader and for the soldiers to bring back a female to the island for studies.

Carlin Eldridge lifted the half-smoked cigar to his lips and smiled wickedly around the tip. He really should give that pride of panthers a break, because Talon Shaw was the one who had opened up the idea for his little project, pulling in millions of dollars by using religion to scare the population into fronting his cause.

"I want you to go in just after midnight," the leader sneered. "Bring me a blonde female if you can find one. I'm thinking about breeding her with this lion we just captured."

The more they studied and bred these abominations, the more money he could get from the followers of his "church." He used that term lightly. Those sheep would follow anything as long as you could turn the good word in your favor.

"Yes, sir," the voice replied.

Chapter Eighteen

Evie bounced on the balls of her feet, shifting from side to side as Kye prepared for their training. Evie watched him as he leaned over to pick up the gloves from his bag. The muscles in his back bunched when he moved, sending heat to her core. Over the last year, Kye had almost doubled in size, making her feel so much smaller than before. His strength was more than just physical, he'd become her biggest supporter and confidant.

Did it really matter that they were not fated to be mates? As sad as she was that they didn't have the spark, she knew she loved him more than her own life. She'd do anything to protect him, and he'd do the same for her.

"Ready?" Kye asked as he turned around, tightening the Velcro on his gloves.

"Yep," she grinned, shaking her arms at her sides to loosen the tension in her body.

The sounds of the woods around her quieted as they began to circle each other. She sized him up, noting how he had grown over the past six months. He was damn near a foot taller than her five-seven frame. He had to weigh two hundred and fifty pounds in muscle. She tipped the scale at one thirty, and she blamed her hips on her genes. The muscles in her arms and legs were all from her training.

"Focus," Kye said, holding his gloves up close to his face. He peered over their tops and shifted to the left. "Are you sure you want to go full out?"

"Yes," she smirked from behind her gloves where he couldn't see her.

With that, Evie threw her first punch, but it was blocked by Kye's beefy gloves. He pulled in his elbows to block a blow to his stomach, making her growl with frustration. Kye got in one good tap to her cheek, but he wasn't hitting hard enough to knock her down.

"Good," he grunted when she moved to the left and repaid him with the same move.

As they sparred, Evie wiped sweat out of her eyes, never looking away from her opponent. It was imperative that she remember her training, not backing down when she would hit him hard enough that Kye would grunt. Every hit she made that sent him a step back only increased her confidence.

"They're coming," Sheriff Lynch barked into the phone.

"When?" Talon gasped.

"On the setting sun tomorrow night," he answered.

"We will be ready," Talon growled, hanging up the phone. He immediately called out to his pride to meet at the circle. It was inevitable… they were going to have to fight.

Chapter Nineteen

Guardians lined up in front of the alpha's home, some of them shifting into their panthers. Others were armed with weapons provided by the sheriff. Evie watched from the window in Talon's office, refusing to hide with the pride females. Hope was by her side, strapped with two guns in her shoulder holster.

"They're going to take me tonight," Evie whispered, looking over at the other female who was already shaking her head in denial.

"We are not going to let them take you," Hope vowed.

"You and I both know the sheriff's visions are solid." Evie blew out a harsh breath. "Hope, I need you to promise me something."

"No," Hope snarled, her eyes glowing amber. "I won't promise you anything, because you aren't going anywhere."

"Just listen to me," Evie snapped, her own panther agitated. "Please keep Kye from hurting himself to come save me. Let the Guardians do it; keep him home."

"That man is going to come after you." Hope raised a brow. "He's growing as an alpha, and I'm fairly certain even his brother's command won't keep him away."

"He's going to try to fight his way to me," Evie acknowledged. "It's going to be dangerous, but I'll be okay."

"You don't know that," Hope reminded her, coming up to pull Evie into a hug. "Please get into the safe room."

"No," Evie replied, looking up into her friend's eyes. Hope had wetness there. Her usual hard shell shattering with worry. Evie started to say something, but gasped when Hope raised her own gun in the air.

"I'm so sorry, but I have to save you," Hope whimpered, bringing the butt of the gun down… making Evie's world go dark.

Evie jumped to her feet, cursing when she looked around the safe room and saw all of the females of the pride with their young. The older couples were consoling everyone as they waited for word of what was happening on the outside. She had a knot on her head from where Hope had struck her. Thankfully, with her fast healing, it was subsiding along with the massive headache from the blow.

"Damn it!" Evie swore, pulling on the door.

"It's for the best," Nova said, holding Atlas to her chest.

"No, it's not," Evie replied, feeling the beast

prowl beneath her skin. She reached for her weapon and threw her hands in the air when she found it gone. "This is bad, Nova... really bad."

"It's for your safety," Liberty repeated to her, handing her sleeping daughter off to Savage's mother.

"No," Evie growled, shifting her eyes as she searched the room. She knew every aspect of the protective space behind the weapons cabinet in the security room, because she helped build and stock it. Reaching above the door, she heard Liberty curse when she retrieved the hidden key. "I'm sorry. I'm going."

"Evie, NO!" Liberty started to grab Evie's hand, but a hard scowl from the young female sent the alpha's mate a step back.

"Do not stop me," she warned as she unlocked the door to her unwanted prison. She slipped out the door, ignoring Noah as he cursed from behind her. She locked the pride in the room and closed the cabinet, tossing the key to the Guardian.

"Where is everyone?"

"Damn it, Evie," Noah shouted, standing up from his seat.

"Noah, I will hurt you if you even try to come at me," Evie warned, her canines thickening in her mouth.

"Shit," he replied, running his hands through his dark hair. "On the lawn. Others are in the woods."

"Kye?" she asked, needing to know where he

was.

Panic lodged in her chest as she felt fear from her leader. Noah spun around and looked at the monitors. Men were coming through the gate at the road with weapons raised. Evie gasped when a human officer was shot.

"The *Community* is here," Noah declared.

"Kye? Where's Kye?" she demanded, scanning the monitors, feeling fear when she didn't see him.

"He's in the woods, not far from our mother's place," Noah replied, changing his tone when she opened the door to the hallway. "You better not get taken!"

She waved him off and hurried out the door, securing it as she left. The alpha's home was dark and silent, as though the home had been abandoned for years. The feeling was strange not seeing people mingling around.

Slipping out the back door, she wanted to cry when she heard gunfire coming from the front lawn. As much as she wanted to run and help the other Guardians, Evie's main focus was finding Kye. She ran across the backyard, past the circle where Talon held their meetings, and headed for the road that led up to the mated cabins.

She partially shifted enough to use her panther's keen sense of smell to find him. It didn't take her long to find his trail.

"Evie!" Kye scolded as she rounded the large

tree close to the small driveway leading to his mother's cabin. "What are you doing?"

"Looking for you," she panted, pushing back her beast.

"You were supposed to be in the safe room," he slipped, cringing when her eyes widened.

"So, you were part of that?" Evie narrowed her gaze and tightened her fists at her sides. Right now, all she wanted to do was clobber Kye and Hope for orchestrating her safety.

"I'm trying to keep you safe," he explained.

"We do this together," she said, poking him in his stupid chest. "I know they are going to come for me, but..."

Her words died in her mouth when a gunshot rang out across the darkness. She screamed when a patch of blood bloomed on Kye's chest. His hands reached for her, but he failed as he gasped for breath... falling to the ground.

"No!" she screamed, her panther ripping from her chest.

When she spun around, there were four males as large as Guardians pointing their weapons at her head. The beast lifted its lip, a vicious snarl rolling off her tongue. The panther backed up, straddling Kye's body as he lay bleeding out on the ground. They weren't going to hurt him anymore as far as she was concerned.

"E...Evie," Kye gasped, gaining her attention.

The human side wanted to shift to give him aide, but her panther won out by dominating to keep her safe. His panther clawed at his human body, attempting to shift to heal himself, but Kye shook his head, fighting the shift. Tears welled up in her eyes when his canines elongated and he snarled, "Run."

Her panther screamed as Kye's body went limp. She jumped for the men, but didn't make it far before one of them raised a hand and a flash of light shot forth from his palm, striking her in the chest. The pain paralyzed her, dropping her body to the ground. Whatever the man had done had forced the shift from her panther back to human.

The men didn't speak as they lifted her from the ground, one of them tossing her limp body over his shoulder like she was nothing more than a flimsy blanket.

Evie tried to scream, but whatever they'd shocked her with kept her from making sounds louder than a simple moan. Reaching down deep, she searched for her beast, but the panther inside her was gone... lifeless.

Talon!
Talon!
Talon!
Nothing.

As she hung over the man's shoulder, Evie felt a lone tear escape her eye. They were going to take her and possibly study her like she was nothing, like she didn't matter.

Gunshots sounded louder as they reached the alpha's home. Still paralyzed, she couldn't move her head to see what was going on, but from the sound of it, her pride was losing the fight. As the man slowed, Evie silently cried out when she saw blood on the ground. Without her beast, she couldn't pick out the scent to know if it belonged to one of her pride or the enemy.

"Get that one in the van," a voice said. "These sons of bitches have more firepower than we thought."

The male grunted and hefted her up higher on his shoulder when he started moving again. As he reached the van, the man turned, and she saw the front lawn of the alpha's home.

It was covered with bodies of Guardians and officers.

Liberty donned the special gloves the females used in training to keep from accidentally touching a male and causing herself pain. It was hard, but she kept the tears out of her eyes as she ran from the closet upstairs, tossing blankets and sheets over the banister to Calla below.

"That's all we have," Liberty yelled. "Start

making pallets on the ground. Use the pillows if you must."

The alpha's living room was a staging area for the wounded. Talon was out with Savage and Winter, looking for Kye, Booth, and Taze. It'd only been half an hour since more deputies from surrounding counties showed up to help them protect the pride. The men were either caught or they committed suicide before they could be taken into custody. The pride took out twelve of them on their own before the mercenaries remaining started opening fire on everyone with semi-automatic weapons.

So many of them had been shot.

Ranger, Lucky, Axel, Diesel, and Kraven were in bad shape. The healer was pulling bullets out of their bodies in preparation for the males to shift to heal. So far, Ranger was the only one alert, and he was fucking pissed.

"Where's my mate?" The male's voice was harsh and deadly. Thankfully, Hope ran from the kitchen with water, sliding to his side. "I'm here. I'm here."

"I need our alpha here," Harold snarled, using long tweezers to dig into Kraven's chest, right above his heart, to find a bullet.

"I'll call for him," Liberty said as she stood back, pressing her hand to her heart. She sent up a silent prayer to whoever was up there listening. *Please don't take any of them from us.*

A commotion on the back porch stopped Liberty

from calling out for her mate. Calla reached for her weapon at the same time Hope stood over her mate protectively. Both females raised their guns toward the door in preparation to shoot the intruder, but when the door flew open, everyone cried out when Kye was brought in naked and bleeding from a wound to the center of his chest.

"*No!*" Liberty's cry was heard throughout the pride, and an agonizing wail echoed from each of them.

Chapter Twenty

They had her tied to the seat in the small plane. It'd been hours since they'd thrown her inside under the cover of darkness, taking off from the small airport in town. There'd been no security around…no one to see her being taken.

She felt the descent and cursed when she caught a glimpse out the window. The sun was just coming up over the horizon when the plane banked to the left, showing her an island in the distance. If that was where they were taking her, she'd have one hell of a time getting away. It didn't matter that her panther loved water, and frequently swam, there was no way she could swim the ocean waters to get to the mainland.

The males surrounded her as soon as the plane landed, one of them removing handcuffs from his back pocket. She looked up into their eyes and frowned when she saw that they were vacant. None of them held any expressions as if they were robots, but she knew they weren't. There was something off about these males… but what?

She was officially scared. Two men held her arms tightly as she was led into a hillside bunker. The walls were concrete and the lights that hung overhead were bright enough to hurt her eyes, but she kept them open to pay attention to her surroundings. She dug deep inside and cried for her alpha, but he never answered.

Talon! Help! Please!

Cries of others could be heard as they moved further into the corridors with doors that were not marked. The males holding her were supernaturally strong, but they were not of her kind. She tried to break free, but the guards only tightened their hold and rushed their steps. The cuffs on her wrists were unlike any she'd used in training. Those she could break with her strength. These felt the same, even weighed the same, but they wouldn't budge.

At the end of the hallway sat a metal door with a small window. When it opened, several men inside turned to look at her. Their faces were covered with masks like her healer wore when he was working on his patients.

"Ah, what do we have here?" one asked as his eyes roamed her body.

"Female black panther," a guard said. "Careful, she's a fighter. Carlin wanted her for mating with a lion."

The guard uncuffed her wrists and pushed her into the arms of the other men, slamming the door behind her. She twisted and kicked out like she'd been trained, knocking one of them to the floor. The second, she punched in the jaw. Her fangs thickened and she pulled at her beast.

Another male shoved her against a wall, but she took that moment to bounce back and attack him. A fist caught her face, spinning the female to the side and directly into the arms of the male who looked at her like she was going to be his next conquest.

Talon!!!

"You cannot call for your leader," the dark-skinned man in the lab coat chuckled. "He's probably dead."

"He's not dead," she spat, hoping to get them to fight her, because she was angry as hell at being taken, again. She knew what to do this time. These men wouldn't hurt her like the wolves had. "I would know if he was."

She would feel the loss of her alpha if he'd died. The feeling was said to be like your chest was being ripped to shreds. She'd been conscious the entire trip to this place. She'd have known if Talon was gone.

Or would she?

She'd been paralyzed by them. Maybe he'd died and she hadn't felt it. Gritting her teeth, Evie knew to not let the enemy get inside her head. She had to think straight.

Focus!

She'd already remembered the path they had taken to get to this room since they entered the underground facility. The one thing that kept her from panicking was knowing that the tracker in her arm was active. They'd be there soon.

The door opened and a large man entered. His gray eyes bounced as he chuckled around a half-smoked cigar, "This one will do. Mate her with that lion."

"Mate me?" she gasped.

"Yeah," the scientist smirked. "Time to see if you all can cross-breed."

"I'll have to reward the warlocks with their choice of a female for bringing me this one," the large man said. Why the hell was he using warlocks? It didn't take but a second for her to realize that was why they'd been so much stronger than her, and the reason why the Watcher could still see them coming. "Maybe they'll borrow this one when you're done with her."

"Not happening," she snarled, putting her left leg forward as she took her stance. "I'll take every single one of you out if you even try to force me to mate."

"You do not scare us," another male replied as the big man left the room, locking the door in his wake. This was the asshole that had punched her when she had tried to fight. The male was big, but nowhere as large as her Guardians. "Even if you did get out of this bunker, you wouldn't be able to get off the island. We have wild shifters out in the forest. They'll do worse than what we are requiring from you."

"Wild shifters?" she questioned, not moving from her position.

"Fucking wolves," he cursed, leering at her body. "They'll like you."

"I'll take my chances," she replied, getting ready to launch herself at the biggest guy in the room and the one who'd struck her when she had arrived. Yeah, he was going out first.

"We'll see," he shrugged, lifting a syringe from the table beside him.

"Not again," she whispered, readying herself for the fight of her life.

Harold wiped his brow and looked up from Talon's baby brother with a grim expression on his face. "I've done all I can."

Talon's mate cried at his side, holding his arm with all of the strength she had left. If it wasn't for her love, he'd have cracked by then. Liberty's strength kept him going as he continued to force his Guardians to shift to save their lives. As he looked around, the ones who were unharmed hovered over the males who were in their panther forms. Some of them slept, others just lay there, panting with exhaustion.

"You need to force his shift," Harold begged. "Kye needs your help, alpha."

Talon pulled in the ancient magic that had been

bred into him by his father. His skin prickled as a cool breeze skirted through his body. His beast was right there, guiding him as he used all of the power he had in his body, directing it toward his baby brother.

"Shift, Kye... shift now!"

Kye's body shivered as his beast fought for release. The shift was slower than usual. Hair sprouted on his brother's body. His ears reshaped. His tail slowly grew to its full length. A low moan escaped the male's lips as his face morphed into that of his cat.

"Kye," Liberty said softly, dropping to her knees beside the panther's head as soon as he'd completed the shift. His brother's beast barely opened its eyes. Talon noticed the amber was fading and tiny blue flecks of his human side were there.

"Do not fight to come back yet," Talon ordered. "You need to heal. We will go get her and bring her home to you."

The panther cackled low in his throat at the alpha's words. It was obvious Kye was at his weakest point. Liberty donned her gloves and stroked Kye's head when a lone tear leaked from the animal's eye. "We *will* bring her home."

Talon turned and focused on the others as he surveyed the chaos that was his home. He couldn't look his brother in the eye anymore and tell him lies to keep him calm.

In all honesty, Talon had no idea when his

Guardians would be healthy enough to go after Evie. He didn't know why he hadn't heard from her yet, either. Garrett had promised she'd call for him, but in his vision, Evie was unable to contact him. They all thought it was because Talon had died.

Well, he was good and alive, and he needed to find his brother's mate.

"Talon," Noah called out from the hallway leading to his office and the security room.

Talon turned at the sound of his brother's voice, using his body to block the sight of their baby brother laying in his own blood. The look on Noah's face was one of fear. "What is it?"

"I've found her," Noah admitted. "And you're not going to like where she is."

Talon moved with speed down the hallway, following his middle brother to the room. When he entered, Noah pointed to the screen. A satellite image was on the larger screen, a blue dot pulsating on a wooded area.

"Zoom out," Talon ordered, his heart thundering in his chest as Noah grabbed the mouse and did as he'd been told. As the image cleared, Talon cursed so loudly, the monitor vibrated. "She's on a goddamn island!"

"I know a guy with a plane," Noah offered, scooping up his phone. "Get the available Guardians armed and ready. I can have them in the air in thirty minutes."

"Do it," Talon ordered.

Chapter Twenty One

Evie spun, her foot connecting with the last scientist's jaw. She felt immense pleasure when he fell limp to the ground. Her heart rate sped as she looked around the room at the four men laying there unconscious. Time was short and she knew she had to get in touch with her pride.

Her hands shook as she searched the males for keys to unlock the door.

She grabbed the syringe from the floor and found its cap on the counter. She pocketed it and moved toward the door. Sliding the key in the hole, she peeked through the tiny window but couldn't see anyone directly in front of the door. She'd have to take her chances with people in the hallway.

"You can do this," she told herself, closing her eyes one more time so she could partially shift.

Talon...Alpha...Please hear me.

It only took a few seconds for him to reply. Evie almost cried with relief when she heard his voice in her head.

The Guardians are on a plane, heading for you.

She pressed a hand to her chest when she felt his strength wrap around her.

I've disabled four scientists, I'm going to fight my way out of this bunker. There is a small runway not far from the entrance.

Evie listened for her alpha to reply, but there was a long pause. She knew he'd probably yell at her and tell her to stay hidden, but she wasn't going to listen to him until he gave the direct order.

Are you hurt?

She assured him that she was fine.

Remember your training, Evie. They are only an hour away.

She swallowed hard, wanting to ask him about Kye, but she was afraid the news was going to be bad. She'd seen him take a bullet to the chest.

He's alive, but very weak. Come home to my brother.

Evie wiped a tear from her cheek and straightened her spine. She had to get back home, but first, she had to shut down the *Community*.

The door let out a soft creak when she slowly opened it. Looking to the right, she noticed the way was clear, but she remembered from paying attention as they brought her in, she needed to go left down the hallway.

She moved with speed as she ran, her eyes set on the door at the end of the corridor. White lights guided her path, doors every few feet were closed, but a sound stopped her in her tracks.

Whimpering and pleas for help reached her ears as she came upon a door several feet from the exit she needed to take. There was a small window, similar to the one in the room she had been held in. As she peeked inside, Evie's beast pushed against her skin for release.

Several cages lined the walls. Shifters in both their human and animal forms were locked inside. The one closest to the door held a female who was laying on her side, panting hard. Evie's eyes scanned the room and saw a male dressed in a lab coat locking her cage. The males in the room were snarling and growling as they yanked on the bars of their cages. The scientist adjusted himself and sneered at the young female. Evie knew immediately what had happened.

She fumbled with the key ring she'd stolen and prayed that the key she chose worked. Sliding it in the lock, she twisted and the lock released. A voice called out from the furthest end of the hallway. When she looked up, another man in a lab coat started running for her.

"Stop!"

Evie pulled the door open and hurried inside, her eyes throwing amber sparks. She quickly closed the door and locked it from the inside. It probably wouldn't stop the guy in the hallway, but it would give her a few minutes to take this son of a bitch out.

"Who are you?" the guy who'd just violated the female barked.

"Your executioner," Evie snarled when she attacked, unleashing her claws and canines as she pounced with the speed of her beast.

The male jumped back, but not far enough for Evie to miss him, and she came down hard enough to knock the male off his feet. Her right hand dug into the soft flesh on his abdomen, her left hand wrapped around his throat.

"I hope you rot in hell," she snarled, squeezing his throat until the man's windpipe was crushed. She used her other hand to rip him to shreds, spilling his organs on the cold tile floor just as Savage had taught her one day in training.

"Who are you?" a male called out from one of the cages.

"My name is Evie, and I am from the Shaw pride," she panted, flipping the keys around on the chain, looking for something that resembled a cage key. "My Guardians are on the way to save us."

"Talon?" another male gasped. "Is your alpha Talon Shaw?"

"Yes," Evie said, looking up at the older male with wide eyes. "Do you know my alpha?"

"His father was my friend," the male said. "My name is Theo McCormick."

Evie found the key to the cages and started unlocking them, waiting to get to the hurt female last. All of the shifters looked up as the door to the room began to shake; the man that had been running down the hallway was yelling something through the window.

"I'm going to get this female, and I need all of you to help me fight our way out of this bunker," Evie commanded, looking over her shoulder at the older alpha. "Are you able to carry her?"

"Give me the woman," Theo ordered.

Evie opened her door and walked inside, holding her hands up. "My name is Evie, and I'm going to get you out of here."

"Did you kill him?" the woman asked, rolling from her side to her knees. She looked horrible. Blood soaked her clothes and her brown hair was a matted mess. Evie swallowed hard, remembering how bad she and Liberty looked when they'd been saved.

"Yes," Evie promised. "We are going to get everyone out."

"Outside?" a young male asked, climbing to his feet as he moved closer to Evie. "There are wolves out there."

"What is your name?" Evie asked, scenting the male was like her, but different. He was some sort of cat.

"My name is Zane," he replied, pushing his long, dark blond hair out of his eyes. The male couldn't have been more than seventeen or eighteen. Evie scented the air again and frowned when he spoke. "I'm a lion, if you're wondering."

"Oh, I didn't know," she apologized. "I've never met anyone like you."

"We are very rare," he explained. "I was

kidnapped from Alaska when they killed my family. As far as I know, I am the only one left."

"I'm so sorry." Evie closed her eyes, begging for the strength to continue on. She had to get these people out of there and pray that her pride was equipped to save everyone. This had to end.

"The wolves are in the woods and they are wild," Zane stated. "I haven't reached my maturity yet, and I cannot compete against them." The boy's face crumbled at his words. Evie could tell he was pissed that he couldn't fight yet. She understood his frustrations more than even he knew.

"I know," Evie said. "We have to get past these guards first. Then we will worry about the wild ones." Evie helped the female up, steadying her as she swayed. It took a moment, but the female gritted her teeth and walked out of her cage.

In all, there was an alpha, the female, a young lion, and two males big enough to be Guardians. The scents around her were confusing. She wasn't quite sure what they were, but it didn't matter, they were all victims, and it was time to get them home.

"Alpha, stay in the middle," Evie ordered, blushing a little. "Sorry, alpha."

"If you know how to get us out of this place," he replied, "I will follow you anywhere, young female warrior."

At that moment, the door burst open and the lab coat guy entered with two males wearing scrubs. Evie and two of the men she'd released dispatched them quickly by snapping their necks. The two males looked at her with respect and pride.

"My name is Shadow," the tall, dark-haired male said. His eyes were golden brown and she figured he was some sort of bear. "This is Santiago." Again, another bear.

"We have to get out of this building and make our way to the small shack not far from the runway. I saw it as they flew me in, but it looks like we have to move through the wooded area for a few hundred yards to get there without using the road. Does anyone know how many wolves are out there?"

"There are six," Theo snarled. "I can command them to stand down, but they fight me. I was forced to give everyone here my blood to keep them from dying. I guess you could say that I'm now the alpha to them all."

"My brother is out there," the female cried. "He isn't a bad male."

"You're a wolf?" Evie gasped, taking a step back. She scented the air, but couldn't scent anything over the female's blood.

"We are not all bad," the woman growled, looking up at Evie with hazy yellow eyes. Evie noticed the woman wasn't as young as she had previously thought. The brighter light in the hallway highlighted her features. "My brother has obeyed Theo."

"What is your name?" Evie asked.

"Luna." She swallowed hard. "My name is Luna Ray."

"Can your brother protect us out there?" Evie questioned, trying to calculate how much time had passed since she'd called out to her alpha.

"Echo will help us," she promised.

"Let's go and make sure we protect the alpha," Evie said as she reached the door to the outside. As they pushed through, the sun blinded the prisoners since they'd been held in cages for so long.

The other males shielded the alpha and Luna as Evie searched for sounds and scents of the enemy, no matter their species. Evie made a hand signal to the people behind her; stay low and quiet. All of them nodded as they entered the wooded area.

Birds flew from their perches in the trees, knowing there were predators around, even if they didn't know how dangerous the shifters in her wake really were. The fact that there were birds in the trees made Evie a little more at ease. If the wolves were around, there would be silence.

Kye shifted again, forced by the power of his brother, his alpha. The pain in his chest was excruciating, and he wished he'd been able to see the men who had grabbed Evie. The only thing pushing him to survive was the knowledge that she would return home to him. The tracking device she'd insisted on having imbedded in her skin was the only thing that would save her now.

His beast protested when Talon forced the animal to recess for the fourth... or was it the fifth time? He didn't know at this point. All he knew was that when he was human, he would shiver and a blanket would cover his naked body. Liberty had held a bottle of water to his lips a few times, wearing special gloves so she could touch him without pain.

"E...Evie," he cried, wanting information on her. Each and every time he was human, he'd call out her name, hoping for someone to talk to him, but all he received was silence. A tear escaped his eye when Liberty came close again with more water. Kye's eyes sparked amber and he stared at his sister-in-law, begging for answers. "Please tell me she's alive."

"She is, but they took her far away," Liberty whispered, stroking his head. "We need you to heal while the Guardians bring her home."

"I...go." He swallowed hard, trying to move, but collapsed back on the mound of blankets they'd put him on in Talon's living room.

"No," Talon growled, kneeling down. His brother rested his hand on Kye's shoulder. The power from his alpha's touch helped ease the pain from his wound, but it didn't heal the pain from the loss of his female. "You have to stay here. You're not in any condition to leave the pride."

"Find… her," Kye begged, releasing his hold on his human side when he felt Talon's power demanding he shift again.

"I promise," Talon whispered as he stood up and walked away.

Chapter Twenty Two

The plane touched down as the sun was setting. Savage, Winter, Booth, Taze, Dane, Storm, and Noah hit the ground as soon as the plane stopped on the small tarmac. Savage's eyes sparked amber as his head raised to the sky, scenting the air.

"Wolves," he snarled, raising his gun. "We need to find Evie, now."

"Aerial maps show a road leading up to the bunker," Noah stated, pulling out a printed overhead picture of the island and pointing to the location they needed to head toward. They were off the fucking coast of Maine. These assholes had found the ultimate bunker to hide out in to conduct their sick and twisted experiments for the sake of learning how the shifters ticked.

"Savage," a female voice called out from his right. When he turned, Evie peeked around a thick tree trunk, her eyes glowing amber.

"Evie," he breathed, breaking off into a dead run for the female. She was covered in blood. "Are you hurt?"

"No," she promised, shaking her head. "I killed some men."

"Jesus," he snarled, knowing she could take care

of herself, but seeing blood on the blue scrubs she was wearing sent his heart into a near panic.

The other Guardians approached, Dane scenting the air. "Evie, we have to move. There are wolves in the area."

"I know," Evie said, holding up her hand. "This is Luna, and she's a wolf. Her brother is out here somewhere, and she promises me that he isn't bad. She isn't either."

A beautiful, brown-haired female, probably around thirty years old, stepped out from behind the tree. She didn't stand with arrogance next to Evie as Savage would've expected. No, she closed in on herself as she hid behind the female.

"She was… she was violated by the scientist that I killed," Evie stated, jutting her chin out. Savage was proud of her, but confused as well. These were wolves.

"We've never found a wolf pack that wasn't feral," Dane stated as his eyes narrowed on Luna. Evie's upper lip vibrated with her snarl as she sidestepped to block them from touching the female wolf. Savage put a hand on Dane's chest, calming the male.

"We need to get you to the plane," Savage ordered.

"My brother is out there," Luna cried, looking over her shoulder. "Theo can control the others. I know he can. I've seen it."

"Wait, Theo?" Winter gasped, pushing past the others. "He's alive?"

"I'm here," Theo rumbled as he came into sight. Three other males flanked him, and from the scent in the air, two of them were bears... grizzly bears. One was something else.

"Lion," Evie chuckled at Savage's surprised reaction.

"How many are there?" Savage turned his question to Evie. He shook off the information about the lion for now.

"Six wolves are in the woods," Theo stated. "One is named Echo, and he's good. The others are wild, and to be honest, I don't know if there is any hope for them."

"We will try to save them," Evie blurted. "We are going to save them all."

They all dropped to their knees when a ball of fire whizzed past them and slammed into the tree trunk Evie had just been standing behind, exploding it into a million pieces. Luna screamed as a sharp spear-like piece cut into her arm.

Theo ran to her side and picked her up as Savage pulled a gun from the holster at his side. Noah and Talon had made sure they were all armed before leaving the pride, because no one knew what the Guardians were walking into on this island.

"Get to the plane!" Taze barked, pointing for Evie and the others to follow him.

They took off at a run, but skidded to a halt not fifty feet from the tree line. Twelve men in all black marched toward them. Each and every one of them held their hands out to their sides… their eyes black as night.

"It's the wizards," Shadow growled. "They're deadly."

"Fuck that," Savage swore, pointing his weapon. One of males lifted his hand, a ball of light rolling and expanding as he raised it over his head. Savage pulled the trigger twice, hitting the male square in the chest, but it did nothing.

"Son of a bitch," Booth cursed, firing his own weapon.

The wizards, or whatever the fuck they were, moved as one toward the plane. Savage knew they had to take them out before they disabled their only way off the island. "Back to the woods! We don't want them taking out the plane."

As one, they ran for the cover of the trees, but it was no use. The males attacked, sending balls of fire in their direction, hitting trees so they'd fall in their path.

"Where are those damn wolves?" Winter hid behind what was left of a tree, ducking low to keep his head clear. He turned to Theo and yelled, "Call them!"

Theo closed his eyes and shook his head. "They are fighting me."

"Fuck," Storm bellowed.

Yips and howls sounded from the other side of the small tarmac where the plane sat in the open as the *Community's* wizards kept coming toward Savage and the others. He prayed those damn wolves would help, or at least slow them down so he could take some of them out. Because at that point, Savage had just about had it with enemies and being fucking shot at.

Luna screamed when one of them turned and threw a fireball toward the wolves, knocking them all to the ground. The agonizing wail from the female shattered his heart. He waited all of two breaths before coming out of his hiding spot to start firing at the wizards. Winter, Taze, and Booth followed his lead. They'd go out in a hail of bullets if that was what it took to get the others off the island. He just prayed his mate and cub would be safe after this. He wasn't sure of himself.

"My brother!" Luna screamed over the gunfire.

"Get back into the trees!" Savage ordered, hoping she'd just fucking listen to him.

"No!" Luna cried, falling to her knees.

"They're coming," Evie called out. Savage took a chance and looked over his shoulder. Evie's eyes were completely shifted, along with part of her face, as she lifted Luna from the ground to move her back to safety. "They're coming!"

Savage had no clue as to what the female was

talking about, but the wicked smile on her face told him she knew something he didn't.

"What the hell are you talking about?" Winter yelled over the sound of weapons being discharged, to no avail. The wizards were immortal.

"Garrett is coming," she cheered. "And he's bringing friends."

A flash of light so bright it turned the world around them white, blinded everyone. When Savage's vision cleared, he couldn't believe what he was seeing before him.

"Holy fuck," Taze gasped. The rumble of disbelief echoed from Savage and the others.

Twenty males appeared, their wings stretched out to touch each other's, making a barrier of protection between the wizards and the shifters. At the head of the group was the sheriff. As soon as their forms solidified, six of them broke off from the crowd and took to the air, coming down at the entrance to the bunker. They entered swiftly, and Savage prayed they were going after whomever was left inside.

"What the hell?" Taze asked. "What are they?"

Two of the angels with Garrett turned their heads, giving the pride a nod before turning around, but not before the shifters noticed the angels had no facial features. All of them, except for Garrett, were missing eyes, noses, and mouths. It was like a white skin covered them, making them nothing but pawns.

"I don't care as long as they're on our side,"

Savage cheered. "Guard the others."

Taze, Booth, Dane, Storm, and Winter regrouped, standing shoulder to shoulder in front of Evie and the others as all hell broke loose. Every time a ball of fire would come from the wizards, the Watchers would move closer, absorbing the glow as it struck their bodies. Savage blinked twice when he saw Garrett grab the ball that'd been aimed at his chest as if it was a solid object and threw it back into the line of the enemy. The male it hit fell to his knees as he grabbed his head, screaming as if he were burning from the inside out.

They went back and forth for several moments, the Watchers were winning until one of the men in black stepped through the line and held his hands in the air. Wind began to blow and limbs from the trees cracked and flew through the air. The angels kept pushing and fighting back, looking as if they were solely focused on their task.

Savage watched as they fought, still not quite believing what he was seeing. He'd never trusted the sheriff, but seeing him come to their aide might just have changed his attitude toward the male.

"What do we do?" Evie asked from behind him.

All of the shifters waited on baited breath as the angels fought back. Savage could only stare at the war between them. It looked like something out of a Hollywood movie where they only used magic to battle.

The sound of helicopters in the distance was barely covered by the angel's destruction of the enemy. As the sound drew closer, the angels fought harder. Savage prayed that whoever was coming was going to help them and not the *Community*.

One by one, the warlocks fell, disappearing as their bodies dropped limply to the ground. Angels began to disappear when their opponent was eradicated. Savage kept looking over his shoulder and cheered to himself when he saw four military helicopters approaching the island.

"It's about fucking time," he snarled, relief flowing through his body. A vision of his mate and cub filtered through his mind as he turned around to look for Garrett. "Where the fuck did they go?"

"They just disappeared," Dane said as he shook his head.

"We should get to the plane," Savage suggested, backing away slowly. He kept his eyes on the scene before him as he herded them back across the small tarmac. Inside the plane, the startled pilot sat there with wide eyes.

A commotion out the window had everyone looking at the bunker doors. Garrett had changed into his sheriff's uniform at some point and was walking out with a team of military men. Savage gasped when he saw the man who'd been the head of the *Community* and the son of a bitch who'd held his mate captive, led out in shackles.

"I could kill him right now," Savage growled, his beast demanding that male's blood.

"We need to go," the pilot hollered over his shoulder. "The military needs this runway."

"Fuck," Savage mumbled under his breath.

"Someone close the door," Booth called out.

"Get this bird prepared to fly," Savage ordered as he gave up his shot at vengeance.

He opened a chest to remove blankets for the female who was still covered in her own blood. She was a wolf, and it went against his nature to help her, but Evie gave her word that this one was good.

He'd be the judge of that.

"The flight is going to take several hours," he grunted. "We will sort everything out when we get back to our home."

"I'm not bad," she said, her eyes glowing from the presence of her beast.

"I'm sorry, but we don't trust wolves," Savage stated.

"I'm a white wolf," she whispered. "I'm different."

"What?" Savage asked, his eyes wide. "There are no white wolves."

"She's not lying," Theo said as he moved closer to the female. "I've seen her. She's not like the others."

"Still don't trust them," Savage replied, his eyes falling on Evie as she checked on the other males she'd rescued. Savage didn't think he'd ever forgive what had happened to her.

Evie covered her body with a scratchy wool blanket that'd been stored in the back of the plane. The ones who had survived the island were silent as the wheels lifted off the ground. Savage and Winter were talking with the pilot while Booth and Dane were checking on everyone else.

"Hey." Booth smiled warmly as he took a seat next to her. He set a bottle of water next to her leg and leaned back against the wall.

"Hey," she replied, blowing out a breath she didn't even know she was holding.

"You do realize that you shut down an entire facility, right?" Booth asked, rolling his head to the side. "You did a good thing."

"Innocent shifters were killed." She shook her head. "I didn't do anything differently than what you or any other Guardian would've done."

"Ranger once said you'd be a voice of change in our world." Booth winked. "I agree."

"I don't want praise," she mumbled, feeling embarrassed. The last thing she wanted was for there to be a big fuss over what she'd done over the past few days.

"Well, you deserve more. I'm proud of the woman you've become." Booth nodded, standing up from his seat. "I have to check on the others."

"Booth... wait!" she called out, reaching out to touch him, but he moved away quickly. Evie frowned when the big Guardian looked at her with wide eyes. "You do know that Kye and I are not mates, right?"

"Doesn't matter," he said with a shrug. The male smiled warmly and ran his hand over his dark, short-cropped hair, his icy blue eyes glowing bright. "He's the mate of your heart, and for that, I will refuse to touch you or allow you to touch me unless you are wearing gloves."

"I can respect that," she answered, hoping things would be okay when she got home. "Thank you."

Booth moved over to check on Luna, dropping his hands at his side when she cowered from his touch. The poor woman was frightened, but she'd helped fight her way off that island despite her brother's death at the hands of the warlocks. The Guardian whispered something to her and moved over to the male bear, Shadow, who'd helped Evie. Booth shook his hand and walked away.

All eyes were on Theo, and Evie was sure everyone wanted to know what was next. Could they all live under his rule like the *Community* had thought? It'd been several weeks since they'd taken the alpha's blood with no signs of weakness. He could command them and they listened, but what would happen after they returned home?

Evie stood on shaky legs and made her way over to the female wolf. It went against her nature to be close to them, but she'd learned that Luna wasn't evil. She wasn't like the ones who'd taken her. No, Luna was different.

"Hey," Evie said as she took a seat next to the female.

"I never thanked you," Luna said, pulling her blanket up over her damaged shoulder.

"There is no need to thank me." Evie frowned. "You're going to be okay. I know it's going to be a long road, but things will get better for you."

"How do you know that?" Luna sniffled.

"I was kidnapped when I was seventeen." Evie heaved a huge breath. "I've learned to live again, and I'm a lot stronger than I was back then."

"I'm so sorry," Luna gasped, reaching out to touch Evie's hand.

"It's okay," Evie promised, feeling closer to the female than she should.

Evie was thankful that Luna didn't press for more information because she didn't want to bring up her time with the wolves. That part was over. Now, she had to worry about Kye and getting home to him so they could start their lives as a mated couple, even if fate hadn't been on their side.

"Our healer will look at that shoulder when we arrive in Mississippi." Evie slowly reached for the blanket and moved it away from Luna's shoulder. The wound had stopped bleeding, but her shoulder was still sliced open. She grabbed more gauze and reapplied a clean dressing, covering the female with the blanket.

"Thank you," Luna sighed. "It's just not healing. I may need to shift."

"Try to rest." Evie smiled, moving back to her seat to wait out her arrival back at the pride. "We will be home soon."

Chapter Twenty Three

Garrett sped up the driveway of the pride, smiling from ear to ear. The *Community* leader was now in custody, and all of his minions were either in a cell next to him or dead. It was finally over, but his job wasn't. The gods should've pulled him, but they hadn't. In his world, that meant there were more threats coming for the Shaw pride.

When Evie called out for him, Garrett used all of his powers to beg the gods for help, and they delivered. He fought alongside others like himself silently as they killed the warlocks. Those warlocks were dark magic and since they were working with the *Community*, Garrett should've been blind, but he wasn't. It didn't take long to realize those magical beings were being forced. Because they were not there willingly, Garrett had to assume that was the reason why his visions were not hindered.

Whatever the answer was, he didn't care. The pride was safe, and Evie was on her way home to her male.

Kye paced in front of the house as the sheriff

arrived, sliding out of his cruiser. The male looked happy, knowing the pride was now safe. The *Community* had been captured and their laboratories were demolished, never to harm their kind again.

"It's over?" Kye asked, wanting to hear it from the Watcher himself.

"It's done," Garrett nodded, looking over his shoulder. "How are you feeling?"

"I'm mostly healed," Kye sighed, not really caring for himself. He wanted to see Evie and make sure she was okay. "Still hurts."

"Evie did great things on that island," Garrett told him. "She'll be here any minute."

"She really is stronger than we all thought," Kye said with pride.

Garrett nodded and walked past him, heading for Talon's office. The pride had all returned to their homes to spend time with their families, and the Guardians who'd been injured were either with their mates or taking some much needed time off at the dorm. Kye, on the other hand, was pushing himself to be upright when his female returned home.

His beast prowled just under his skin as he waited. Each second was as agonizing as the gunshot he took to the chest. He'd been shifting nonstop for the past twenty-four hours, and while he needed to shift a few more times, he'd deal with that later.

Kye released a heavy breath when vehicles drove toward the alpha's home, one of them carrying his female. His need for her was a heavy feeling in his heart. The only thing that kept him alive during those first hours after she'd been taken by the enemy was knowing she was unharmed when the Guardians had arrived on that island.

Kye waited patiently when he saw her step out of the black SUV, taking a moment to thank the gods she was alive. Savage spoke softly to her, and on Evie's nod, she looked up to see him standing on the front porch. He took the steps one at a time, wanting to run to her, but he didn't.

"Hey," she breathed, tears filling her eyes. "Are you okay?"

"I'm fine, baby," he replied, reaching up to touch her cheek, but she pulled away, causing his beast to snarl. "What?"

"I need to change." She cringed, looking down at the dried blood on her clothes. Evie wiped the wetness from her eyes and clenched her teeth. Kye knew she was trying to be brave, but would probably break down once they were alone. He didn't fault her for holding on to her strength.

"Who's blood is that?" he snarled, his eyes glowing amber.

"Not mine," she assured him, looking behind her as the others exited the vehicles. Kye had no desire to meet the ones they'd saved. All he wanted was to be with her. "Can we just go home so I can shower?"

"Let's go," he agreed. "We can come back and

check in with Talon after you are taken care of. I should feed you, too."

"Food sounds amazing," she groaned, turning on her heel to walk up the road that led to their cabin. "I can make my own. You're still healing."

"I'm healed enough," he growled.

Once inside, she left him sitting on the couch so she could shower. His panther urged him to go after her; to bathe her... his mate. The need to check her over from head to toe was strong, and he pushed his beast back, knowing she needed some space.

They needed to start their life together, regardless of them not being fated mates. He'd had a lot of time to think about their relationship while he was healing. He'd been through every emotion. Did he let her go? Did he fight for her to belong to him forever?

"Kye," she whispered from the doorway. He scented her tears before he saw them spill over her cheeks. He stood and walked slowly toward her, waiting for her to reach out for him. He wanted nothing more than to tuck her against his body and shield her from the cruel world she'd been in over the past few years, but he didn't.

"I love you, Evie," he said, holding open his arms. "You are so strong and have proved you can do anything. I am so proud of the woman you've become. Now, let me hold you."

It took her two steps to reach him... and when he cupped her face, something happened.

"Oh," Evie gasped, her eyes glowing amber as her canines pushed through her gums.

The air around them changed, an invisible thread twined around their hearts, making them beat as one.

"Finally," he snarled as he took her lips. Their canines clashed as they came together, not able to separate for fear of losing the moment. His cock hardened painfully as their beasts made themselves known, snarling at the need to mate… to complete the bonding they'd been denied on her birthday.

"Mate," she cried. "We are mates."

"Yes, we are, baby," he grinned, picking her up so he could carry her to the bedroom.

He didn't even turn off the lights as he made his way to the bed. Evie ripped at her nightshirt, revealing she was bare underneath. Kye's beast prowled inside, pushing against his human skin. The need for her was unbearable.

"On your knees," he demanded, forgetting his own pain so he could mate his female officially and for good.

Evie scrambled up on her knees, lowering her chest to the bed. She turned her face so she could breathe. Kye wasted no time in entering her from behind, pulling her long hair so his chest would meet her back. With his free hand, he cupped her breast and rolled her nipple between his fingertips, relishing in her soft moans.

"You are mine, always." He struck the spot on

her neck that he'd bitten on her birthday. Her rich blood entered his mouth and he swallowed, keeping his hold on her while he thrust in hard jerks.

"Don't stop, Kye," she begged, her hand reaching back to squeeze the top of his thigh.

A powerful urge to release inside her overpowered him, her scent growing with each thrust. His panther was in control as he continued to thrust. God, she smelled of sunshine and something sweet. Something more appealing than anything he'd ever known came from her skin.

"Your scent has changed," he growled as he released her, lapping over the mark.

"Fuck," she cried. "I feel different, Kye. I… I think I'm fertile."

"Jesus," he cursed, pushing her back so she was flat on the bed once again. His hand curled around her hips as he thrust repeatedly, knowing that he had to finish inside her to complete them.

"I need to mark you." Evie's voice was mumbled as she cried into the bedsheets.

As her panther nature took over, Evie bucked against him, dislodging him from her body. The snarl of her panther echoed in the room as she pushed him over, throwing a leg over his body. Her strong yet tiny hands wrapped around his cock. She pumped it twice before guiding it back to her sex. With a curse, Evie seated herself atop him, her hands falling on his chest, right above where he'd been shot.

"Mark me, my mate," he demanded, his head lifting from the pillow.

Evie wasted no time in placing a hand on his head, pushing it to the left. His only warning was a deep inhale from her before she struck.

"*Fuck*," he yelled when her sharp canines buried deep. His body gave up and released inside her, marking their final act to become bonded mates.

Harold looked up at the female through his dark lashes, knowing he had to abide by his code as a healer to give her aide, but it went against everything he knew about wolves to accept that she was actually *good*.

"W…What are you going to do to me?" she stuttered, obviously scared out of her mind. The female was still covered in blood and the gods only knew what else from that island. All Harold could tell was that Luna had to be close to thirty years old, even though she was the size of a young female.

"You will be checked out and then released to go on about your way," Harold stated. His stoic voice was a clear indication that he wanted to keep her far away from his pride.

"With Theo?" she sniffled, brushing her dirty, brown hair away from her face. She needed a bath.

"With whomever you please." He shrugged, reaching for his special gloves. "You are not a prisoner here, but you cannot stay, either."

"Where's the alpha?" she blurted as Harold approached. The female scooted up the exam table and pulled her tiny legs closer to her chest, attempting to protect herself. "I want my alpha."

"He's in a meeting with my alpha, Talon," Harold said, coming to her side. "I need to see what the scientists did to you and make sure there is no damage."

"N…no," she whimpered, large pools of tears welling up in her yellow eyes. "Please… Please don't."

"I'm not going to hurt you," Harold vowed, taking two steps away from the female. Fuck! What was he thinking? It didn't matter that she was the enemy. This female had been violated in the worst way possible, then stuck in a foreign pride of panthers and their healer. She was expected to just let Harold tend to her in a room closed off to the only person she trusted… her alpha; a man who wasn't even her kind.

The entire situation was a mess.

"I will wait to examine you until Theo returns," the healer relented, "but you have to tell me what happened to you. I need to know where you are hurt."

"I hurt in my soul," Luna said, covering her face as she continued to cry. "I have nothing left."

"Wait a minute," he said under his breath. Harold

took his rolling stool and moved it close to her, but not close enough to make her uncomfortable. "You have Theo."

"I only have him because they made me take his blood," she replied. "I don't even know if he wants a band of shifter misfits under his rule. If he doesn't, I will die because I don't know of any other white wolves. They killed all the ones I knew."

"Don't speculate anything until Theo comes back from talking to Talon," Harold replied, hoping he could put her at ease long enough for him to look her over. "Would you feel better if you had a shower? I have some scrubs you can wear."

"I would like that very much, thank you," she replied.

Harold walked over to a door and opened it wide to reveal a bathroom. He pointed to the cabinet with the clean towels and left the room, finding his office chair and the cup of tea that had gone cold when the new arrivals entered his home.

He didn't know how Theo was going to control a group of shifters unlike his own kind. Two bears, a lion, and a white wolf. Who would've known that *any* alpha could keep them alive with just his blood? That had never happened before, and no one knew of any mixed groups in their histories. If it had happened before, no one had known.

Of course, before their reveal to the humans, most groups kept to themselves, only crossing paths as they traveled in ancient times. Some, like Theo and Talon's father, worked together because of business needs.

The phone on his desk rang, and he picked it up to hopefully hear some good news from someone in his pride.

"Hello?"

"Harold?" Evie said from the other line. Her voice was a little unsteady.

"Evie," he paused, "How are you?"

"Good… I think," she whispered. "Can I ask you something without having to come into your office?"

"Of course," he replied, his mind churning over a thousand different reasons why she'd be calling… all of them bad.

"Well, I haven't told anyone this," she said. "Kye and I are finally mates."

"That's wonderful news!" he cheered, but he fell silent when his enhanced hearing picked up the sound of her breath catching. "What else, Evie?"

"I went into heat tonight," she answered.

"Okay," he drawled. "How long ago?"

"About an hour ago," she answered. "I don't think I'm with child, though."

"Give it time," he told her, hoping she was just being paranoid, but in all reality, the young female would probably never produce offspring. "Try to rest, and when you wake up in the morning, you will know… your mate will know."

"Thank you," she said, hanging up as quickly as she had called.

Harold's head jerked up at the scent that filtered through his home. Something sweet and a bit wild tickled his nose, and his beast roared beneath his skin. Before he could rise from his chair to follow the scent, Luna appeared in the doorway, wearing a pair of blue scrubs. Her hair fell in ringlets over one shoulder and she was stunningly beautiful.

"Thank you for the shower," she blushed.

"Um," he cleared his throat, "Um, yeah. You're welcome. Are you ready for me to exam you?"

"Yes... no, maybe?" She hesitated. "Honestly, healer, the thought of another man touching me makes me want to claw my skin off, but I have some medical training from my pack, and I know you need to check me. Can you just make it quick?"

"I can," he said with a nod. "However, it may be better if we get Theo here to be outside the room."

"I'll go back to the exam room." She frowned, lowering her head.

The thought of those scientists hurting any female sent him into a rage, but why did the knowledge of the things they had done to Luna make him want to find them all and kill them with his bare hands?

Evie's eyes fluttered open as the sun was rising over the horizon. She was warm all over and quickly realized Kye had not left her side the entire night. His large body was wrapped around hers in his sleep.

She took stock of her body, hoping to feel differently, maybe even a bit sick, but was disappointed when there was nothing. Their mating night was perfect, and the fact that she'd actually gone into heat was a blessing. The realization that she didn't conceive had her eyes watering.

"Why are you crying?" Kye mumbled in his sleep. How did he know she was crying?

"Go back to sleep," she cooed, rubbing circles over the back of his hand where it rested against her empty womb.

She waited several minutes for his breathing to even out before slipping from the bed. Inside the bathroom, she stood in front of the mirror and examined the mating mark on her neck. The two marks were scarred and stood out brightly against the light over the sink.

Evie rested her hands on the sink and lowered her head. The healer had been right. She would probably never carry a cub for her mate.

"How can I help him lead a pride with no chance of giving him an heir?" she whispered.

"I will never lead a pride," he spoke from the door, startling Evie so much that she fell into a defensive stance as she spun around to meet him. She didn't even hear him get out of bed.

"What?"

"When I was dying…" he paused to reach out for her. She went to him willingly, resting her head on his massive chest. "I realized that I didn't want to rule a pride. My life is with you, Evie."

"But you are an alpha," she mumbled against his skin.

"Only by blood, but not by mind," he said, shrugging. "Can I just want to live a peaceful life with my mate?"

"You don't care that I didn't conceive last night?" she sniffled, feeling more tears fill her eyes.

"We just mated, baby," he replied, tucking his finger under her chin so she'd look up at him. When their gazes connected, she saw love, compassion, and pride in his. "We have all the time in the world to make a family."

"What if we never do?"

"Then I will love you enough to fill that void," he said truthfully, capturing her lips. He scooped her up and took her back to their mated bed, showing Evie all the ways she was loved by the male who'd always been destined to be her forever.

The End…
Look for The Healer's story coming soon…

About Theresa Hissong:

Theresa is a mother of two and the wife of a retired Air Force Master Sergeant. After seventeen years traveling the country, moving from base to base, the family has settled their roots back in Theresa's home town of Olive Branch, MS, where she enjoys her time going to concerts and camping with her family.

After almost three years of managing a retail bookstore, Theresa has gone behind the scenes to write romantic stories with flare. She enjoys spending her afternoons daydreaming of the perfect love affair and takes those ideas to paper.

Look for other exciting reads…coming very soon!

Need more Paranormal Romance?
Follow the VC Warriors in "The Protectors Series" by
Teresa Gabelman
New York Times & USA Today Best Selling Author

| Book 1 | Book 2 | Book 3 | Book 4 | Book 5 | Book 6 |

| Book 7 | Book 8 | Book 9 | Book 10 | Book 11 |

Lee County Wolves **More Vampires** **Contemporary**

www.TeresaGabelman.com

Made in the USA
Lexington, KY
24 April 2018